The Call of The Wild

*A Rugged Survival Epic of Instinct,
Loyalty & the Savage Beauty of
the Wilderness*

A Modern Translation
Adapted for the Contemporary Reader

Jack London

Translated by Tim Zengerink

Table of Contents

Preface
Message to the Reader

Rebuilding the Greatest Library in Human History

Thousands of years ago, the Library of Alexandria was the heart of global knowledge — a sanctuary where the wisdom of every known civilization was gathered and shared freely.

And then, it was lost.

Now, we're rebuilding it — and you are invited to join us.

At the Library of Alexandria, we've set out to make every book available to every person on Earth — not just in print, but in every language, every format, and for every reader.

Here's how we do it:

- **Deluxe Print Editions at True Printing Cost** - Order any book as a high-quality paperback, elegant hardcover, or stunning boxset — and only pay what it costs to print. No markups. No middlemen.
- **Unlimited Access to the Greatest Works** - Enjoy thousands of timeless classics — from Plato to Shakespeare to Tolstoy — in beautiful, modern eBook and audiobook editions. Read and listen without limits — for every reader, everywhere.
- **Modern Translations for Every Language & Dialect** - We're reimagining the classics in clear, accessible language — and translating them into every dialect imaginable. Everyone deserves to understand humanity's greatest ideas.

When you visit **LibraryofAlexandria.com**, you're not just accessing books — you're joining a global movement to restore, preserve, and share the wisdom of civilization.

Join us today at LibraryofAlexandria.com

Together, we'll ensure the light of human wisdom never fades again.

With gratitude,

The Modern Library of Alexandria Team

Visit:
www.libraryofalexandria.com
Or scan the code below:

Introduction

From Domestication to Destiny: The Return to Primal Truth in Jack London's Masterpiece

In a time when civilization continues to stretch its borders and technology further insulates humanity from the natural world, Jack London's *The Call of the Wild* remains a powerful reminder of our deep and ancient connection to nature, struggle, and instinct. First published in 1903 during a period of American expansionism, industrial ambition, and a romantic fascination with the frontier, London's novel endures not just as an adventure story, but as a philosophical meditation on identity, freedom, and the primal essence that lies dormant in every living being.

The Call of the Wild is often remembered for its gripping narrative—a tale of a domestic dog named Buck, stolen from his life of comfort in California and thrust into the brutal world of the Yukon during the Klondike Gold Rush. Yet beneath its surface-level adventure is a far deeper journey: the story of a creature's reawakening to its own raw and unfiltered truth. Through violence, loss, loyalty, and elemental hardship, Buck is transformed. What begins as a tale of survival evolves into a spiritual odyssey—a journey backward through evolution, into instinct, into the wild.

Jack London, drawing from his own experiences in the Yukon and his lifelong fascination with social Darwinism, Nietzschean philosophy, and the raw power of nature, crafts a narrative that is both epic and intimate. Buck's story is not simply the story of a dog. It is an allegory for the human soul's yearning for authenticity, the struggle against societal constraint, and the inevitable call of the deeper self—untamed, unbroken, and true.

In this introduction, we will explore the historical context in which London wrote, the philosophical underpinnings of the novel, the literary techniques that give it such visceral power, and the ways in which *The Call of the Wild* continues to resonate with readers today. It is a work that, like the wilderness itself, refuses to be tamed—offering not comfort, but clarity. Not escape, but confrontation with what is most essential in us all.

Evolution, Conflict, and the Return to Instinct

Jack London's vision of life was shaped by the rugged experiences of his youth—working-class hardships, seafaring voyages, and an insatiable appetite for adventure. In the late 1890s, he joined the Klondike Gold Rush in the Yukon Territory. Though he found no fortune there, he discovered something more valuable: the raw material for some of the greatest fiction in American literature. The wilderness of the North, with its deadly cold, its indifference to human ambition, and its brutal yet beautiful landscapes, left an indelible mark on London's imagination. It became not only the setting but the crucible for his most enduring ideas.

The Call of the Wild emerges directly from this crucible. At its core, it is a tale of evolution—not in the strictly biological sense, but in the philosophical sense of transformation and self-recovery. Buck, a domesticated St. Bernard-Scotch Collie mix, begins the novel as a privileged house pet, pampered and protected in Judge Miller's estate in California. His theft and subsequent journey into the Arctic act as the inciting trauma that sets him on a path of regression—or, as London would argue, progression—into his authentic, ancestral self.

This return to instinct is not romanticized. Buck suffers. He is beaten, starved, overworked, and forced to fight for dominance among other dogs. He witnesses cruelty in humans and indifference in nature. And yet, through this suffering, Buck awakens. Each challenge strips away the layers of his domestication. He learns the "law of club and fang." He learns how to steal for survival, how to lead a pack, how to obey his instincts when the civilized mind would hesitate.

London's use of third-person limited narration allows the reader to inhabit Buck's thoughts without anthropomorphizing him. Buck does not reason like a human; he feels, intuits, senses—qualities that London elevates as vital to true existence. The more Buck listens to these impulses, the stronger and more autonomous he becomes. In the wild, he does not descend into savagery. He ascends into sovereignty.

The conflict of the novel is not simply between Buck and his environment—it is between the constraints of man-made systems and the freedom of natural law. Civilization, with its comforts and rules, is shown to weaken the soul. The wilderness, with its dangers and purity, is where character is forged and destiny fulfilled. Buck's call is not toward chaos but toward order—a deeper, older order governed by instinct, balance, and respect for the power of nature.

This message, grounded in London's reading of Darwin, Nietzsche, and Herbert Spencer, resonates today more than ever. In a world where many live disconnected from the earth, from hardship, and from self-reliance, Buck's journey becomes a metaphor for reclaiming what is vital: courage, presence, and primal clarity.

The Tragedy and Triumph of Transformation

While *The Call of the Wild* is often seen as an adventure story, it is also profoundly tragic. Buck's transformation is purchased at a steep cost. He loses everything: his home, his innocence, his companions, and the final thread of human connection he cherishes most—John Thornton.

Thornton is the one human character in the novel who treats Buck with love and respect. Their bond is deep and spiritual, transcending the master-pet dynamic. But even this relationship, pure as it is, cannot anchor Buck to the human world forever. When Thornton dies—killed by brutal Native raiders in a moment of senseless violence—Buck is released entirely. No more obligations. No more ties. He answers the call at last, vanishing into the wilderness, running with the wolves, becoming legend.

This ending is both mournful and victorious. Buck has become who he was meant to be—but only after enduring the full weight of grief and loss. London is not offering an escapist fantasy. He is offering a harsh truth: transformation requires sacrifice. Freedom requires solitude. To become wild again is to give up not just comfort, but connection. And yet, in that loss, there is a greater gain—the reclamation of soul.

Buck's final metamorphosis is symbolic of the human condition. The world teaches us to conform, to obey, to submit to systems and expectations. But somewhere inside, London suggests, there is a deeper call—a call to rise, to hunt, to create meaning not from approval but from authenticity. Buck is not just a dog. He is the spirit of rebellion, of self-actualization, of return.

The literary power of the novel lies in London's ability to make this transformation feel real. His prose is muscular, rhythmic, and evocative. The Yukon is not just described— it is lived. You feel the snow under Buck's paws, the cold in your bones, the adrenaline of the chase. London does not just tell you a story. He immerses you in it. His style is both economical and poetic, delivering high emotion without sentimentality, and philosophical insight without abstraction.

This combination of narrative immediacy and thematic depth is what makes *The Call of the Wild* such a rare achievement. It speaks to readers across ages and cultures because it touches something universal: the yearning to break free, to find purpose, to return to the source of life and know it fully.

Why Buck Still Howls: The Modern Relevance of a Wild Soul

More than a century after its publication, *The Call of the Wild* remains one of the most widely read and frequently adapted works in American literature. Its appeal spans generations— from schoolchildren discovering the thrill of adventure to adults confronting the existential weight of identity and transformation. In Buck's journey, each reader finds a reflection of their own.

In an era of screens, cities, and simulated realities, the novel's message is both countercultural and essential. It reminds us that beneath our technology, our habits, and our distractions, we are still animals—thinking, feeling, sensing beings meant to move, to adapt, to struggle, and to grow. It invites us to listen for the call beneath the noise—the whisper of instinct, the pull of challenge, the desire to run free.

Jack London wrote at a time of immense transition—when the frontier was closing, and America was redefining itself. His work captures the tension between progress and loss, between domestication and freedom. In doing so, he offers not answers, but direction. He does not romanticize suffering, but he does affirm its value. He does not promise peace, but he does promise truth.

The Call of the Wild is not a tale to be tamed. It is meant to unsettle, to inspire, and to awaken. It asks each of us: What part of you has been caged by convenience? What part longs to break free? What will you become if you listen—to the silence, to the wind, to the wild?

Let this novel guide you through those questions. Let it remind you that survival is not just about staying alive. It is about becoming alive. And that, sometimes, begins with answering the call. You are not alone in hearing it. Buck heard it too. And he ran. So might you.

Chapter I:
Into the Primitive

"Ancient wandering desires surge forward,
Straining against the bonds of convention;
Once more from its winter slumber
Awakens the wild, untamed nature."

Buck didn't read the newspapers, or he would have realized that trouble was coming, not just for him, but for every coastal dog with strong muscles and thick, long fur, from Puget Sound all the way down to San Diego. Men searching through the Arctic darkness had discovered gold, and steamship and transportation companies were promoting this discovery, causing thousands of people to rush north. These men needed dogs, and the dogs they needed were large, powerful animals with strong muscles for hard work and thick coats to shield them from the freezing cold.

Buck lived at a large house in the sunny Santa Clara Valley. It was called Judge Miller's place. The house sat back from the road, partially concealed among the trees, through which you could catch glimpses of the wide, cool veranda that wrapped around all four sides. Winding gravel driveways led to the house, curving through expansive lawns and beneath the intertwining branches of tall poplar trees. Behind the house, everything was even more impressive than what you could see from the front. There were enormous stables where a dozen grooms and stable boys worked, rows of vine-covered servants' cottages, a vast and well-organized collection of outbuildings, long grape arbors, green pastures, orchards, and berry patches. There was also the pumping station for the artesian well, and the large concrete tank where Judge Miller's boys took their morning swim and cooled off during hot afternoons.

Buck ruled over this vast estate. This was where he was born, and where he had spent all four years of his life. Of course, there were other dogs around. On such an enormous property, there had to be other dogs, but they didn't matter. They came and went, living in the crowded kennels, or staying hidden in the corners of the house like Toots, the Japanese pug, or Ysabel, the Mexican hairless— odd creatures that hardly ever stuck their noses outside or stepped onto the ground. Then there were the fox terriers, at least twenty of them, who barked threatening promises at Toots and Ysabel as they watched from the windows, safely protected by an army of housemaids carrying brooms and mops.

Buck wasn't just a house dog or a kennel dog. The entire estate belonged to him. He dove into the swimming pool or went hunting with the Judge's sons; he accompanied Mollie and Alice, the Judge's daughters, on long evening or early morning walks; on winter nights he rested at the Judge's feet in front of the crackling library fireplace; he gave the Judge's grandsons rides on his back, or tumbled with them in the grass, and watched over them during their wild adventures down to the fountain in the stable yard, and even further, where the pastures and berry patches were. He moved among the terriers with commanding authority, and he completely disregarded Toots and Ysabel, because he was the ruler—ruler over every creeping, crawling, and flying creature on Judge Miller's property, humans included.

His father, Elmo, a massive St. Bernard, had been the Judge's constant companion, and Buck seemed destined to follow in his father's footsteps. He wasn't quite as large— he weighed only one hundred and forty pounds—because his mother, Shep, had been a Scottish sheepdog. Still, one hundred and forty pounds, combined with the dignity that comes from comfortable living and widespread respect, allowed him to carry himself with truly regal bearing. During the four years since he was a puppy, he had lived the life of a well-fed aristocrat; he took great pride in himself and was even somewhat conceited, as country gentlemen sometimes become due to their isolated circumstances. However, he had redeemed himself by avoiding becoming just a spoiled house pet. Hunting and similar outdoor activities had kept the excess weight off and strengthened his muscles; and for him, like those who take cold baths regularly, the love of water had served as both a stimulant and a way to maintain good health.

This was the kind of dog Buck was in the fall of 1897, when the Klondike gold rush pulled men from around the globe into the frozen North. However, Buck didn't read newspapers, and he had no idea that Manuel, one of the gardener's assistants, was bad company. Manuel had one major flaw. He was passionate about playing the Chinese lottery. Furthermore, when it came to gambling, he had one fatal weakness—he believed in a betting system; and this guaranteed his downfall. Playing a system demands money, but a gardener's assistant's wages barely cover the expenses of supporting a wife and many children.

The Judge was attending a meeting of the Raisin Growers' Association, and the boys were occupied with organizing an athletic club on the unforgettable night when Manuel betrayed them. Nobody witnessed him and Buck leaving together through the orchard on what Buck believed was simply a casual walk. Except for one lone man, nobody saw them reach the small flag station called College Park.

This man spoke with Manuel, and money changed hands between them.

"You should probably wrap up the merchandise before you hand it over," the stranger said roughly, and Manuel looped a thick piece of rope around Buck's neck beneath his collar.

"Twist it, and you'll choke him plenty," said Manuel, and the stranger grunted a ready affirmative.

Buck had accepted the rope with calm dignity. Certainly, this was an unusual situation, but he had learned to trust the men he knew and to believe they possessed wisdom beyond his own understanding. However, when the rope's ends were handed to the stranger, he growled threateningly. He had simply expressed his dissatisfaction, believing in his pride that showing displeasure was enough to take control. But to his shock, the rope tightened around his neck, cutting off his air. In sudden fury, he lunged at the man, who met him partway, grabbed him firmly by the throat, and with a skillful twist flipped him onto his back. Then the rope constricted ruthlessly while Buck thrashed in rage, his tongue hanging from his mouth and his massive chest heaving uselessly. Never in his entire life had he been treated so brutally, and never in his entire life had he felt such anger. But his strength faded, his eyes grew dim, and he lost consciousness as the train was stopped and the two men hurled him into the baggage car.

The next thing he knew, he became vaguely aware that his tongue was in pain and that he was being bounced around inside some sort of vehicle. The rough blast of a train whistle signaling a crossing told him exactly where he was. He had traveled with the Judge too many times not to recognize what it felt like to ride in a baggage car. He opened his eyes, and they filled with the wild fury of a kidnapped

11

king. The man lunged for his throat, but Buck was faster. His jaws clamped down on the man's hand, and he didn't let go until his consciousness was choked away once again.

"Yes, he has seizures," the man said, concealing his injured hand from the baggage handler, who had been drawn by the sounds of the struggle. "I'm taking him up to San Francisco for the boss. There's an excellent veterinarian there who thinks he can cure him."

Regarding that night's journey, the man defended himself most persuasively in a small shack behind a bar on the San Francisco waterfront.

"All I get is fifty for it," he grumbled; "and I wouldn't do it over for a thousand, cold cash."

His hand was bandaged with a blood-soaked handkerchief, and his right pant leg was torn from the knee down to the ankle.

"How much did the other guy get?" the bar owner demanded.

"A hundred," came the response. "I wouldn't accept a penny less, I swear."

"That makes a hundred and fifty," the bar owner calculated; "and he's worth it, or I'm an idiot."

The kidnapper unwrapped the bloody bandages and examined his torn hand. "If I don't get rabies—"

"It's because you were born to be hanged," laughed the bar owner. "Here, give me a hand before you take off," he added.

Stunned and enduring unbearable agony in his throat and tongue, with his life nearly choked away, Buck tried to confront those tormenting him. However, he was knocked down and strangled over and over again, until they managed to file off the heavy brass collar from around his neck. After that, the rope was taken away, and he was thrown into a cage-like crate.

There he remained for the rest of the exhausting night, brooding over his anger and hurt pride. He couldn't comprehend what any of it meant. What did these unfamiliar men want from him? Why were they confining him in this cramped cage? He didn't understand the reason, but he felt weighed down by an unclear feeling that something terrible was about to happen. Multiple times throughout the night he jumped to his feet when the shed door creaked open, hoping to see the Judge, or at least the boys. But every time it was the round face of the saloon-keeper that looked in at him through the pale glow of a tallow candle. And every time the happy bark that formed in Buck's throat turned into a fierce growl.

But the saloon-keeper left him alone, and the next morning four men came in and lifted the crate. Buck figured these were more tormentors, since they looked like evil characters—rough and dirty—and he snarled and raged at them through the bars. They just laughed and jabbed sticks at him, which he immediately attacked with his teeth until he understood that this was exactly what they wanted. So he lay down in a sullen mood and let them lift the crate into a wagon. Then he, along with the crate that held him prisoner, began a journey that would pass him through many different hands. Workers at the express office took control of him; he was wheeled around in another wagon; a truck transported him, along with various boxes and packages, onto a ferry boat; he was trucked off the ferry into a massive railway station, and eventually he was placed in an express car.

For two days and nights, this freight car was pulled behind screaming locomotives, and during those two days and nights, Buck didn't eat or drink anything. When the railroad workers first tried to approach him, he responded with angry growls, so they decided to torment him in return. Whenever he threw himself against the metal bars, shaking and foaming at the mouth, they would laugh and mock him. They made growling and barking sounds like horrible dogs, meowed like cats, and flapped their arms while making rooster calls. Buck understood it was all foolish behavior, but this made it even more insulting to his pride, and his rage continued to build and intensify. The hunger didn't bother him as much, but being without water caused him terrible pain and pushed his fury to an extreme level. Given his high-strung and sensitive nature, the cruel treatment had made him feverish, a condition that worsened due to the swelling and dryness in his throat and tongue.

He felt relieved about one thing: the rope was no longer around his neck. That rope had given them an unfair advantage, but now that it was gone, he would prove himself to them. They would never manage to get another rope around his neck again. He was absolutely determined about that. For two days and nights he refused to eat or drink anything, and during those two days and nights of suffering, he built up such intense anger that it spelled trouble for whoever crossed him first. His eyes became bloodshot, and he transformed into a furious beast. He had changed so dramatically that even the Judge wouldn't have been able to recognize him, and the mail carriers felt a wave of relief when they loaded him off the train in Seattle.

Four men carefully lifted the crate from the wagon and carried it into a small backyard surrounded by high walls. A heavy-set man wearing a red sweater that hung loose around his neck came outside and signed the delivery book for the driver. Buck sensed that this was the man who would be his next tormentor, and he threw himself violently against the bars of his cage. The man gave a grim smile and picked up a hatchet and a club.

"You're not going to take him out now?" the driver asked.

"Sure," the man replied, driving the hatchet into the crate to pry it open.

The four men who had carried it in immediately scattered in all directions, and from their safe positions on top of the wall, they got ready to watch what would happen next.

Buck lunged at the breaking wood, driving his teeth deep into it, pushing and fighting against it. Every spot where the hatchet struck from the outside found him there on the inside, snarling and growling, as desperately eager to escape as the man in the red sweater was methodically determined to free him.

"Now, you red-eyed devil," he said, after he had created an opening large enough for Buck's body to pass through. At the same time, he dropped the hatchet and moved the club to his right hand.

Buck was truly a wild, furious beast as he prepared to attack, his fur standing on end, foam dripping from his mouth, and a crazed gleam in his bloodshot eyes. He hurled his one hundred and forty pounds of rage directly at the man, fueled by the bottled-up fury of two days and nights. While airborne, just as his jaws were about to clamp down on the man, he felt a jarring blow that stopped his body mid-flight and snapped his teeth together with excruciating force. He tumbled through the air, crashing to the ground on his back and side. He had never been hit with a club before and couldn't comprehend what had happened. With a growl that was partly a bark and mostly a shriek, he sprang to his feet and leaped into the air once more. Again the stunning blow came and sent him crashing violently to the earth. This time he realized it was the club striking him, but his rage ignored all sense of caution. Time after time he attacked, and each time the club stopped his charge and knocked him to the ground.

After receiving a particularly brutal strike, he struggled to his feet, too stunned to charge forward. He stumbled weakly around, blood streaming from his nose, mouth, and ears, his magnificent fur splattered and spotted with crimson foam. Then the man stepped closer and intentionally delivered a devastating blow to his nose. All the suffering he had previously experienced was nothing compared to the intense agony of this strike. With a roar that was nearly as fierce as a lion's, he launched himself at the man once more. But the man, switching the club from his right hand to his left, calmly grabbed him by the lower jaw, simultaneously twisting downward and backward. Buck spun a full circle through the air, and halfway through another, before slamming into the ground on his head and chest.

For the final time, he charged forward. The man delivered the calculated blow he had deliberately held back for so long, and Buck collapsed and fell to the ground, completely unconscious.

"He's really good at training dogs, that's what I'm saying," one of the men on the wall shouted enthusiastically.

"I'd rather break wild horses any day, and twice on Sundays," was the reply of the driver, as he climbed onto the wagon and started the horses.

Buck's awareness gradually returned, though his physical strength remained absent. He remained motionless where he had collapsed, observing the man wearing the red sweater from his position on the ground.

"'Responds to the name Buck,'" the man said to himself, reciting from the saloon owner's letter that had announced the shipment of the crate and its contents. "Well, Buck, my boy," he continued in a friendly tone, "we've had our little fight, and the best thing we can do is leave it at that. You've learned where you stand, and I know where I stand. Be a good dog and everything will go smoothly and life will be good. Be a bad dog, and I'll beat the stuffing out of you. Do you understand?"

As he spoke, he fearlessly patted the head he had beaten so ruthlessly, and although Buck's fur instinctively bristled at the touch of the hand, he tolerated it without objection. When the man brought him water, he drank thirstily, and afterward he quickly devoured a large meal of raw meat, piece by piece, from the man's hand.

He had been defeated (he understood that much); but his spirit remained unbroken. He realized, once and for all, that he had no hope of winning against a man wielding a club. He had absorbed this harsh lesson, and throughout the rest of his life he would never forget it. That club served as an eye-opening revelation. It marked his introduction to the rule of primitive law, and he accepted this introduction without resistance. Life's realities took on a more brutal character; and though he confronted this harsh reality without fear, he faced it with all the dormant cleverness of his nature awakened. As time passed, other dogs arrived, some in wooden crates and others at the ends of ropes, some submissively, and others snarling and howling just as he had arrived; and, without exception, he observed them all fall under the control of the man in the red sweater. Repeatedly, as he witnessed each savage demonstration, the lesson became deeply ingrained in Buck's mind: a man with a club served as a lawmaker, a master who must be obeyed, though not necessarily appeased. Buck never stooped to this latter behavior, although he did witness defeated dogs that groveled before the man, wagging their tails and licking his hands. He also witnessed one dog that refused to either appease or obey, ultimately killed in the battle for dominance.

From time to time, strangers would arrive and speak with the man in the red sweater in various ways— sometimes with excitement, sometimes trying to persuade him. During these encounters, Buck noticed money changing hands, and afterward the strangers would leave with one or more dogs. Buck couldn't help but wonder what happened to those dogs since they never returned, but a deep fear about his own future weighed heavily on him, and he felt relieved each time he wasn't chosen.

Yet his time came, in the end, in the form of a little withered man who spoke broken English and many strange and crude exclamations which Buck could not understand.

"Holy cow!" he shouted when he spotted Buck. "That's one hell of a dog! Hey? How much?"

"Three hundred, and that's a gift," the man in the red sweater replied immediately. "And since it's government money, you can't complain about it, can you, Perrault?"

Perrault smiled broadly. Given that dog prices had skyrocketed due to the extraordinary demand, it wasn't an unreasonable amount for such an excellent animal. The Canadian Government wouldn't lose money on the deal, and their mail deliveries wouldn't be delayed. Perrault understood dogs well, and when he examined Buck, he recognized that this was an exceptional specimen—"One in ten thousand," he thought to himself.

Buck watched money change hands between them, and he wasn't surprised when both Curly, a friendly Newfoundland, and he were taken away by the small, withered man. This was the final time he would see the man in the red sweater, and as he and Curly gazed at Seattle growing smaller from the deck of the Narwhal, it was also his last glimpse of the warm Southland. Perrault took Curly and him below deck and handed them over to a dark-skinned giant named François. Perrault was a French-Canadian with dark skin, but François was a French-Canadian mixed-blood who was twice as dark. These men represented a new type of human to Buck, and he would encounter many more like them in the future. Although he never developed any fondness for them, he gradually came to genuinely respect them. He quickly discovered that both Perrault and François were just men who remained calm and fair when dispensing justice, and they possessed too much knowledge about dogs to be deceived by canine tricks.

In the lower deck of the Narwhal, Buck and Curly met two other dogs. One was a large, snow-white dog from Spitzbergen who had been taken by a whaling captain and later joined a Geological Survey expedition into the Barrens. He appeared friendly, but in a deceptive way, grinning at you while planning some sneaky trick, like when he stole food from Buck's dish during their first meal. When Buck lunged forward to punish him, François's whip cracked through the air, striking the thief first, leaving Buck only able to retrieve his bone. Buck thought this was fair of François, and the half-breed started to earn Buck's respect.

The other dog didn't make any friendly gestures, nor did he welcome any from others; he also didn't try to steal from the new arrivals. He was a gloomy, sullen character, and he made it clear to Curly that all he wanted was to be left alone, and furthermore, that there would be serious trouble if he wasn't left alone. They called him "Dave," and he ate and slept, or yawned in between, showing no interest in anything, not even when the Narwhal crossed Queen Charlotte Sound and rolled and pitched and bucked like something possessed by demons. When Buck and Curly became excited, nearly wild with terror, he lifted his head as if irritated, gave them an uninterested look, yawned, and fell asleep again.

Day and night the ship pulsed with the relentless rhythm of the propeller, and while each day seemed much like the last, Buck could sense that the weather was getting steadily colder. Finally, one morning, the propeller fell silent, and the Narwhal buzzed with excitement. Buck felt it, just as the other dogs did, and understood that something was about to change. François put them on leashes and led them up to the deck. The moment Buck stepped onto the cold surface, his paws sank into something white and slushy that felt much like mud. He jumped back with a sharp snort. More of this white substance was drifting down from the sky. He shook it off, but more kept landing on him. He sniffed at it with curiosity, then licked some with his tongue. It stung like fire, and in the next moment it vanished. This confused him. He tested it again, getting the same result. The people watching burst into loud laughter, and he felt embarrassed, though he couldn't understand why, since this was his first encounter with snow.

———————————

Chapter II:
The Law of Club and Fang

Buck's first day on the Dyea beach felt like a living nightmare. Every single hour brought fresh shock and surprise. He had been violently torn away from the center of civilized life and thrown into the raw heart of primitive existence. This wasn't the comfortable, leisurely life he had known, where he could simply relax in the sunshine with nothing to do but rest and feel restless. Here there was no peace, no rest, and not even a moment of safety. Everything was chaos and constant movement, and at every instant his life and body were at risk. He desperately needed to stay alert at all times, because these dogs and men weren't the tame dogs and people from town. They were all wild creatures who recognized no rules except the brutal law of violence and teeth.

He had never witnessed dogs fighting the way these wolf-like creatures battled, and his first encounter provided him with an unforgettable lesson. It's true that this was an indirect experience, otherwise he wouldn't have survived to learn from it. Curly became the victim. They had set up camp near the log store, where she, in her good-natured manner, approached a husky dog that was the size of a mature wolf, although not nearly as large as she was. There was no advance warning, just a lightning-fast leap forward, the sharp snap of teeth meeting flesh, an equally quick retreat, and Curly's face was torn open from her eye down to her jaw.

It was the wolf's way of fighting—strike and then leap away—but there was much more happening here. Thirty or forty huskies rushed to the scene and formed a tight, silent circle around the fighters. Buck couldn't understand their quiet intensity or the eager way they licked their lips in anticipation. Curly charged at her opponent, who struck her again and jumped back. When she rushed him the next time, he met her attack with his chest using a strange technique that knocked her completely off her feet. She never got back up. This was exactly what the watching huskies had been waiting for. They swarmed over her, growling and howling, and she disappeared beneath the writhing mass of bodies, screaming in pain.

The attack happened so quickly and without warning that Buck was completely stunned. He watched Spitz stick out his red tongue in that mocking way he had when he found something amusing, and he saw François grab an axe and leap into the chaotic pile of fighting dogs. Three men carrying clubs rushed to help him break up the pack. The whole thing was over fast. Within two minutes of Curly hitting the ground, the last of her attackers had been beaten away with clubs. But there she remained, motionless and dead in the blood-soaked, trampled snow, her body practically ripped apart, while the dark-skinned mixed-race man stood above her, swearing viciously. This horrific scene would return to haunt Buck's dreams again and again. So this was how things worked here. There was no such thing as fair fighting. Once you were knocked down, it was all over for you. Well, he was determined to make sure he never fell. Spitz stuck out his tongue and laughed once more, and from that instant forward, Buck despised him with an intense and eternal hatred.

Before he had recovered from the shock of Curly's tragic death, he was hit with another shock. François strapped a harness of leather and buckles onto him. It was the same type of harness he had watched the stable hands put on horses back home. Just as he had seen horses work, he was now put to work, pulling François on a sled into the forest that bordered the valley, then returning with loads of firewood. Although his pride was deeply wounded by being turned into a work animal, he was smart enough not to fight back. He threw himself into the work with determination and gave his best effort, even though everything was completely new and unfamiliar. François was strict, expecting immediate obedience, and his whip ensured he got it; meanwhile Dave, an experienced wheel dog, would bite Buck's hindquarters whenever he made a mistake. Spitz served as the lead dog and was equally experienced, and though he couldn't always reach Buck, he would growl sharp corrections from time to time, or cleverly shift his weight in the harness to pull Buck in the right direction. Buck was a quick learner, and with the combined teaching from his two teammates and François, he made impressive progress. By the time they returned to camp, he had learned to stop at "ho," to move forward at "mush," to take wide turns around bends, and to stay clear of the wheel dog when the loaded sled came racing downhill behind them.

"Three very good dogs," François told Perrault. "That Buck, he pulls like hell. I teach him quick as anything."

By afternoon, Perrault, who was eager to get back on the trail with his dispatches, came back with two more dogs. He called them "Billee" and "Joe," two brothers who were both genuine huskies. Even though they were sons of the same mother, they were as different as day and night. Billee's only flaw was that he was too good-natured, while Joe was completely the opposite—bitter and withdrawn, always snarling with hostile eyes. Buck welcomed them in a friendly way, Dave paid no attention to them, while Spitz went ahead and beat up first one, then the other. Billee wagged his tail trying to make peace, started to run when he realized that trying to appease Spitz wouldn't work, and whimpered (still trying to be peaceful) when Spitz's sharp teeth cut into his side. But no matter how Spitz moved around him, Joe spun on his feet to face him, his fur standing up, ears flattened back, lips curled and snarling, jaws snapping together as quickly as he could manage, and eyes glowing with evil intent—he was the perfect example of aggressive fear. His appearance was so frightening that Spitz had to give up on punishing him; but to hide his own embarrassment, he turned on the harmless and crying Billee and chased him to the edge of the camp.

By evening Perrault found another dog, an old husky that was long, lean, and gaunt, with a face marked by battles and a single eye that flashed a warning of skill that demanded respect. His name was Sol-leks, which means the Angry One. Like Dave, he asked for nothing, gave nothing, and expected nothing; and when he walked slowly and purposefully into their group, even Spitz stayed away from him. He had one unusual trait that Buck was unfortunate enough to discover. He didn't like being approached on his blind side. Buck unknowingly made this mistake, and his first indication of his error came when Sol-leks spun around and slashed his shoulder down to the bone for three inches in both directions. From that moment on, Buck stayed away from his blind side, and for the rest of their partnership had no further problems. His only visible goal, like Dave's, was to be left alone; though, as Buck would later discover, each of them had one other and even more important ambition.

That night Buck faced the major challenge of finding a place to sleep. The tent glowed warmly with candlelight against the white landscape, and when he naturally walked inside, both Perrault and François pelted him with angry words and kitchen tools until he snapped out of his shock and ran shamefully back into the freezing cold. A bitter wind was blowing that stung him harshly and attacked his injured shoulder with particular cruelty. He lay down in the snow and tried to sleep, but the cold soon had him shaking as he got back on his feet. Wretched and hopeless, he roamed around the various tents, only to discover that every spot was just as freezing as the next. Occasionally fierce dogs charged at him, but he raised the hair on his neck and growled menacingly (since he was learning quickly), and they allowed him to continue on his way without bothering him.

Finally an idea occurred to him. He would go back and check on how his own teammates were doing. To his surprise, they had vanished. Once more he wandered through the massive camp, searching for them, and once more he came back empty-handed. Could they be inside the tent? No, that wasn't possible, or he wouldn't have been forced out. So where on earth could they be? With his tail hanging low and his body trembling, looking utterly miserable, he walked aimlessly around the tent. All at once the snow collapsed beneath his front paws and he dropped down. Something moved under his feet. He jumped back, his fur standing on end and growling, afraid of whatever unseen and unknown thing lurked there. But a friendly little bark put him at ease, and he moved back to take a closer look. A breath of warm air drifted up to his nose, and there, tucked under the snow in a cozy ball, was Billee. He whimpered apologetically, squirmed and wiggled to demonstrate his friendly intentions, and even dared, as an offering of peace, to lick Buck's face with his warm moist tongue.

Another lesson. So that's how they did it, right? Buck confidently chose a spot, and with a lot of commotion and wasted energy began to dig a hole for himself. In an instant the warmth from his body filled the enclosed space and he fell asleep. The day had been long and exhausting, and he slept deeply and peacefully, though he growled and barked and struggled with nightmares.

He didn't open his eyes until the sounds of the awakening camp stirred him. Initially, he couldn't figure out where he was. Snow had fallen throughout the night, and he was completely covered. The snow walls surrounded him from all directions, and a powerful wave of terror rushed through him—the terror of a wild creature caught in a snare. This reaction showed he was reaching back through his own existence to the experiences of his ancestors; after all, he was a domesticated dog, an extremely domesticated dog, and from his personal experience had never encountered a snare and therefore couldn't naturally fear one. The muscles throughout his entire body tightened suddenly and automatically, the fur on his neck and shoulders bristled upward, and with a savage growl he leaped straight up into the brilliant daylight, snow swirling around him in a sparkling cloud. Before his paws touched the ground, he spotted the white camp stretched out in front of him and recognized where he was and recalled everything that had happened from the moment he went for a walk with Manuel to the hole he had carved out for himself the previous night.

A shout from François greeted his appearance. "What did I tell you?" the dog-driver called out to Perrault. "That Buck will definitely learn as quickly as anything."

Perrault nodded seriously. As a messenger for the Canadian Government, carrying important official documents, he was eager to obtain the finest dogs, and he was especially pleased to have acquired Buck.

Three more huskies joined the team within an hour, bringing the total to nine dogs, and in less than fifteen minutes they were harnessed and heading up the trail toward Dyea Canyon. Buck felt relieved to be leaving, and although the work proved demanding, he discovered he didn't really hate it. The enthusiasm that energized the entire team and spread to him caught him off guard; even more startling was the transformation he witnessed in Dave and Sol-leks. They had become completely different dogs, utterly changed by wearing the harness. Their previous indifference and detachment vanished entirely. They became sharp and energetic, determined that the work should proceed smoothly, and became intensely agitated by anything that caused delays or confusion and slowed their progress. The strain of pulling in the traces appeared to represent the ultimate purpose of their existence, the sole reason they lived and the only source of their joy.

Dave was a wheel dog or sled dog, with Buck pulling directly in front of him, followed by Sol-leks; the remaining members of the team were arranged in single file ahead of them, leading up to Spitz, who served as the lead dog.

Buck had been deliberately positioned between Dave and Sol-leks so he could learn from them. He was a quick learner, and they proved to be equally effective teachers, never letting him stay confused for long and reinforcing their lessons with sharp bites. Dave was fair and very intelligent. He never bit Buck without good reason, and he never hesitated to bite him when correction was needed. Since François's whip supported their discipline, Buck discovered it was better to improve his behavior than to fight back. During one short stop, when he became tangled in the harness and delayed their departure, both Dave and Sol-leks attacked him and gave him a thorough beating. The tangle that resulted was even worse, but Buck made sure to keep the traces untangled from then on. By the end of the day, he had become so skilled at his work that his teammates almost stopped bothering him. François's whip cracked less often, and Perrault even showed Buck respect by picking up his feet and examining them closely.

It was a grueling day's journey, up through the Canyon, past Sheep Camp, beyond the Scales and the tree line, across glaciers and snow drifts that were hundreds of feet deep, and over the massive Chilcoot Pass, which separates the salt water from the fresh water and stands as a forbidding guardian to the melancholy and isolated North. They made excellent time traveling down the series of lakes that fill the craters of long-dead volcanoes, and late that evening they arrived at the enormous camp at the head of Lake Bennett, where thousands of gold prospectors were constructing boats in preparation for the spring ice breakup. Buck dug his sleeping spot in the snow and fell into the deep sleep of the utterly exhausted, but far too soon he was awakened in the frigid darkness and strapped into his harness alongside his teammates to pull the sled.

That day they covered forty miles on a well-packed trail, but the following day, and for many days after that, they had to break their own path through the snow, which meant working much harder while making slower progress. Typically, Perrault walked ahead of the dog team, using snowshoes to pack down the snow and make the going easier for them. François, who steered the sled using the gee-pole, occasionally switched positions with him, though this didn't happen very often. Perrault was in a rush, and he took great pride in his understanding of ice conditions, knowledge that proved essential since the autumn ice was extremely thin, and in areas where the water flowed rapidly, there was no ice whatsoever.

Day after day, without end, Buck labored in the harness. They always broke camp before dawn, and by the time the first pale light appeared in the sky, they were already on the trail with fresh miles stretching behind them. They invariably set up camp after nightfall, consuming their small portion of fish before burrowing into the snow to sleep. Buck was constantly starving. His daily ration of a pound and a half of dried salmon never seemed like enough. He was never satisfied and endured constant hunger. Meanwhile, the other dogs, who were lighter and naturally suited to this harsh life, received only one pound of fish each day yet somehow maintained their strength and health.

He quickly abandoned the refined habits that had defined his previous life. Once a picky eater, he discovered that his companions, who finished their meals first, would steal his leftover food. There was no way to protect it. While he fought off two or three dogs, the remaining food would vanish down the throats of the others. To solve this problem, he ate as quickly as they did; and hunger drove him so powerfully that he didn't hesitate to take what wasn't his. He observed and absorbed these lessons. When he witnessed Pike, one of the newer dogs who was a cunning shirker and thief, secretly snatch a piece of bacon while Perrault wasn't looking, he copied the act the next day, making off with an entire chunk. This caused a tremendous commotion, but no one suspected him; meanwhile Dub, a clumsy fool who always got caught, received punishment for Buck's crime.

This first theft showed that Buck was capable of surviving in the harsh northern wilderness. It demonstrated his ability to adapt and adjust to new circumstances—without this flexibility, he would have faced quick and brutal death. The theft also revealed the breakdown of his moral character, which had become useless baggage in the merciless fight for survival. Back in the South, where love and companionship ruled, it made sense to respect other people's property and feelings. But here in the North, where violence and savagery dominated, anyone who worried about such things was a fool, and following those old principles would only lead to failure.

Buck didn't think this through logically. He was simply adapting, and without realizing it, he adjusted himself to this new way of living. Throughout his entire life, regardless of how difficult the situation, he had never backed down from a fight. However, the club wielded by the man in the red sweater had instilled in him a more basic and primal set of rules. When he was civilized, he would have been willing to die for a moral principle, such as defending Judge Miller's riding-whip; but the extent of his return to wildness was now shown by his ability to run away from defending a moral principle in order to save his own skin. He didn't steal because he enjoyed it, but because his stomach demanded it. He didn't take things openly, but stole in secret and with cunning, out of fear of the club and sharp teeth. In short, he did what he did because it was simpler to do these things than to avoid doing them.

His transformation happened quickly, though it could be seen as either progress or decline. His muscles turned as hard as steel, and he became immune to ordinary pain. He developed efficiency both inside and outside his body. He could consume anything, regardless of how disgusting or difficult to digest it might be; and once consumed, his stomach acids extracted every last bit of nutrition from it.

His bloodstream then carried these nutrients to every corner of his body, creating the strongest and most durable tissues possible. His vision and sense of smell became extraordinarily sharp, while his hearing grew so sensitive that even while sleeping, he could detect the slightest noise and determine whether it signaled safety or danger. He mastered the technique of using his teeth to remove ice that formed between his toes, and when he needed water but found a thick layer of ice covering the water source, he would shatter it by standing up and hammering it with his rigid front legs. His most notable characteristic was his ability to detect wind patterns and predict them a full day ahead. Regardless of how still the air seemed when he created his sleeping spot near a tree or embankment, the wind that eventually came always found him positioned on the sheltered side, protected and comfortable.

And he didn't just learn through experience—ancient instincts that had been dormant for generations suddenly came back to life. The effects of domestication stripped away from him. In unclear but powerful ways, he remembered back to when his breed was young, to the era when wild dogs traveled in packs through ancient forests and hunted down their prey on the run. Learning to fight with slashing attacks and quick wolf-like snaps came naturally to him. This was exactly how his long-forgotten ancestors had fought. They awakened the primitive life that lay dormant within him, and the ancient techniques that had been embedded in his breed's genetic memory became his own techniques. These abilities came to him effortlessly, without any need to figure them out, as if they had always belonged to him. And when he lifted his nose toward a star on quiet, freezing nights and let out long, wolf-like howls, it was his ancestors—long dead and turned to dust—who were pointing their noses at stars and howling across the centuries through him. And the rhythm of his howls matched theirs, the same rhythms that had expressed their sorrow and what the harshness, cold, and darkness meant to them.

As a sign of how much life resembles a puppet show, the ancient song flowed through him and he reclaimed his true nature; and this happened because men had discovered gold in the North, and because Manuel was a gardener's assistant whose pay couldn't cover the expenses of his wife and several small versions of himself.

Chapter III:
The Dominant Primordial Beast

The powerful primitive instinct was strong in Buck, and under the harsh conditions of life on the trail it continued to grow stronger. However, this growth remained hidden. His newly developed cleverness gave him balance and self-control. He was too occupied with adapting to his new existence to feel comfortable, and he not only refused to start fights, but he stayed away from them whenever he could. A certain carefulness marked his behavior. He wasn't inclined toward reckless and hasty actions; and despite the intense hatred between him and Spitz, he showed no impatience and avoided all aggressive behavior.

On the other hand, perhaps because he sensed Buck was a dangerous rival, Spitz never missed a chance to bare his teeth. He would even go out of his way to intimidate Buck, constantly trying to provoke the fight that could only end with one of them dead. This confrontation might have happened early in the journey if not for an unexpected accident. At the end of that day, they set up a harsh and miserable camp on the shore of Lake Le Barge. Blowing snow, a wind that sliced like a blazing knife, and darkness forced them to fumble around looking for a place to camp. They couldn't have found worse conditions. Behind them rose a sheer rock wall, and Perrault and François had no choice but to build their fire and lay out their sleeping bags on the lake's frozen surface. They had left their tent behind at Dyea to keep their load light. A handful of driftwood sticks gave them a fire that melted down through the ice, leaving them to eat their evening meal in complete darkness.

Close beneath the protective rock, Buck created his sleeping spot. The place was so cozy and warm that he didn't want to leave when François handed out the fish he had warmed by the fire. However, when Buck finished eating and came back, he discovered someone else in his nest. A threatening growl revealed that the intruder was Spitz. Up until this moment, Buck had stayed away from conflict with his enemy, but this crossed the line. The wild animal inside him erupted. He launched himself at Spitz with such fierce anger that it caught both of them off guard, especially Spitz, since everything he had learned about Buck suggested that his rival was an unusually fearful dog who could only stand his ground because of his impressive weight and size.

François was also surprised when they burst out in a tangled mess from the destroyed nest, and he understood what had caused the problem. "A-a-ah!" he shouted to Buck. "Give it to him, by God! Give it to him, the dirty thief!"

Spitz was just as ready for the fight. He was howling with pure fury and anticipation as he moved in circles, looking for an opening to attack. Buck was equally eager and just as careful, also circling around as he searched for the upper hand. But that's when something unexpected occurred, something that would push their battle for dominance far into the future, beyond countless exhausting miles of travel and hard work.

A curse from Perrault, the thunderous sound of a club striking against a skeletal body, and a piercing cry of agony announced the eruption of chaos. The campsite was suddenly found to be swarming with sneaking furry shapes—starving huskies, eighty or a hundred of them, who had caught the scent of the camp from some nearby Indian village. They had slipped in while Buck and Spitz were battling, and when the two men jumped among them with heavy clubs they bared their fangs and fought back fiercely. They were driven wild by the aroma of food. Perrault discovered one with its head plunged deep into the food box. His club struck hard against the thin ribs, and the food box was knocked over onto the ground. Immediately twenty of the starved animals were clawing and fighting for the bread and bacon. The clubs beat down on them without effect. They cried out and wailed under the shower of strikes, but continued to struggle just as frantically until every last morsel had been consumed.

Meanwhile, the startled sled dogs had rushed out of their shelters only to be attacked by the savage intruders. Buck had never encountered dogs like these before. It looked as if their bones might break through their skin. They were nothing but skeletons, loosely covered in matted fur, with burning eyes and drooling fangs. However, their starvation-driven madness made them frightening and unstoppable. There was no way to resist them. The sled dogs were immediately pushed back against the cliff during

34

the first attack. Buck found himself surrounded by three huskies, and within moments his head and shoulders were torn and cut open. The noise was terrible. Billee was whimpering as he always did. Dave and Sol-leks, bleeding from numerous wounds, were fighting courageously together. Joe was snapping his jaws like a wild beast. At one point, his teeth clamped down on a husky's front leg, and he bit straight through the bone. Pike, who usually avoided work, jumped on the injured animal, snapping its neck with a swift bite and twist. Buck grabbed a foaming enemy by the throat and was splattered with blood as his teeth pierced the jugular vein. The warm flavor of blood in his mouth drove him to become even more savage. He threw himself at another dog, and simultaneously felt teeth pierce his own throat. It was Spitz, attacking him treacherously from the side.

Perrault and François, after clearing their section of the camp, rushed to rescue their sled dogs. The wild surge of starving animals retreated before them, and Buck broke free from the chaos. However, this freedom lasted only briefly. The two men were forced to rush back to protect their food supplies, which allowed the huskies to resume their assault on the team. Billee, his terror transforming into courage, burst through the vicious circle and escaped across the ice. Pike and Dub raced after him, with the remaining team members close behind. As Buck prepared to leap after them, he caught sight of Spitz charging toward him from the corner of his eye, clearly intending to knock him down. If he fell beneath that pack of huskies, he would have no chance of survival. He steadied himself against the impact of Spitz's attack, then joined the escape across the lake.

Later, the nine sled dogs came together and found refuge in the forest. Although no one was chasing them, they were in terrible condition. Every single dog had wounds in four or five different places, and some had been hurt very badly. Dub had a serious injury to his back leg; Dolly, the last husky who had joined the team at Dyea, had her throat badly torn; Joe had lost one of his eyes; and Billee, who was usually so gentle and friendly, had his ear chewed and shredded to pieces, and he cried and whined all through the night. When morning came, they slowly and carefully limped back to their camp, only to discover that the attackers had left and the two men were in foul moods. More than half of their food supplies had been taken. The wild huskies had gnawed through the ropes that held the sled together and torn through the canvas covers. In reality, they had devoured anything that could possibly be eaten, no matter how unlikely it seemed as food. They had consumed a pair of Perrault's moccasins made from moose hide, bitten off chunks from the leather harness straps, and even eaten two feet of the leather cord from the tip of François's whip. He stopped staring sadly at the damaged whip and turned his attention to examining his injured dogs.

"Ah, my friends," he said softly, "maybe it will make you a mad dog, all those bites. Maybe we're all mad dogs, damn it! What do you think, eh, Perrault?"

The courier shook his head with doubt. With four hundred miles of trail still stretching between him and Dawson, he couldn't afford to have his dogs go crazy. Two hours of swearing and hard work got the harnesses back in order, and the injured, stiff team started moving again, fighting their way painfully over the most difficult section of trail they had faced so far, and indeed, the toughest stretch that lay between them and Dawson.

The Thirty Mile River stretched wide and open before them. Its turbulent waters resisted the freezing temperatures, with ice forming only in the calm eddies and sheltered spots. It took six grueling days of backbreaking work to traverse those thirty brutal miles. The journey was truly harrowing, as every single foot of progress put both dogs and men in mortal danger. Time and again, Perrault, who was leading the way and testing the route, crashed through the fragile ice bridges, only surviving because of the long pole he carried, which he positioned so it would fall across the opening created by his falling body each time he broke through. A severe cold front had moved in, with the thermometer showing fifty degrees below zero, and every time he plunged through the ice, he had no choice but to stop and build a fire to dry his clothes, as his very survival depended on it.

Nothing could intimidate him. His fearless nature was exactly why he had been selected as a government courier. He willingly took every kind of risk, boldly pushing his small, weathered face into the bitter cold and pressing forward from the faint light of dawn until darkness fell. He traveled along the threatening shorelines on thin ice that flexed and snapped beneath his feet, ice so dangerous they couldn't afford to stop. On one occasion, the sled crashed through the ice with Dave and Buck, and they were nearly frozen solid and almost drowned before they could be pulled to safety. The customary fire became essential for their survival. They were completely encased in ice, and the two men forced them to keep running in circles around the fire, making them sweat and gradually thaw out, staying so close to the flames that they got scorched by the heat.

At another time, Spitz broke through the ice, pulling the entire team behind him toward Buck, who fought desperately to pull backward with every ounce of strength he had, his front paws gripping the slick edge while the ice trembled and cracked all around them. But Dave was behind him, also straining backward with all his might, and behind the sled stood François, pulling so hard his tendons felt ready to snap.

Once more, the ice along the edge cracked and fell away both in front of them and behind them, leaving no way out except to climb up the steep rock face. Perrault managed to scale it through what seemed like a miracle, while François prayed desperately for exactly that kind of miracle to happen. Using every leather strap, sled rope, and the remaining pieces of harness tied together into one long rope, they pulled the dogs up one by one to the top of the cliff. François climbed up last, coming after the sled and its cargo had been hauled up. Then they had to find a spot where they could climb back down, which they eventually accomplished with the help of the rope, and when night fell they found themselves back on the river having gained only a quarter of a mile for the entire day's effort.

By the time they reached the Hootalinqua and found solid ice, Buck was completely exhausted. The other dogs were in the same condition; but Perrault, trying to make up for lost time, drove them from early morning until late at night. On the first day they traveled thirty-five miles to the Big Salmon; the following day they covered another thirty-five miles to the Little Salmon; on the third day they went forty miles, which brought them close to the Five Fingers.

Buck's paws weren't as tough and hardened as those of the huskies. His had grown soft over countless generations since his last wild ancestor had been domesticated by a cave dweller or river dweller. Throughout each day he hobbled in pain, and once camp was set up, he collapsed like a lifeless dog. Despite his hunger, he wouldn't move to get his portion of fish, forcing François to bring it directly to him. The dog driver also massaged Buck's paws for thirty minutes every evening after dinner, and gave up the leather from his own moccasins to craft four protective coverings for Buck's feet. This brought tremendous relief, and Buck even managed to make Perrault's weathered face break into a smile one morning when François forgot the moccasins and Buck rolled onto his back, waving all four paws pleadingly in the air, refusing to move without them. Eventually his paws toughened up from the trail, and the worn-out footwear was discarded.

At the Pelly one morning, while they were getting the harnesses ready, Dolly, who had never stood out for anything special, suddenly went mad. She revealed her condition with a long, heart-wrenching wolf howl that made every dog's hair stand on end with fear, then lunged straight at Buck. He had never witnessed a dog lose its mind, and he had no experience with madness to make him afraid; still, he recognized that this was something terrible, and he ran from it in sheer panic. He raced away immediately, with Dolly gasping and foaming at the mouth just one bound behind him; she couldn't catch up to him because his terror was so intense, but he couldn't escape her because her madness drove her relentlessly forward. He crashed through the forested center of the island, rushed down to the far end, crossed a back channel packed with jagged ice to reach another island, made it to a third island, curved back toward the main river, and in his desperation began trying to cross it. Throughout this entire chase, even though he didn't turn to look, he could hear her growling just one leap behind him. François shouted to him from a quarter mile away, and he turned back, still maintaining his one-leap advantage, breathing heavily and struggling for air while putting all his trust in François to rescue him. The dog-driver raised his axe and held it ready, and as Buck raced past him, the axe came crashing down on mad Dolly's head.

Buck stumbled against the sled, completely drained, gasping for air, unable to defend himself. This was exactly the chance Spitz had been waiting for. He lunged at Buck, and his teeth bit down twice into his defenseless enemy, tearing through flesh all the way to the bone. Then François's whip came down, and Buck felt satisfied watching Spitz get the most severe beating that had ever been given to any dog on the team.

"That Spitz is one devil," Perrault remarked. "Some damn day he's going to kill that Buck."

"That Buck is two devils," François replied. "All the time I watch that Buck, I know for sure. Listen: some damn fine day he's going to get mad as hell and then he's going to chew that Spitz all up and spit him out on the snow. Sure. I know."

From that moment forward, it became an all-out war between them. Spitz, serving as the lead dog and recognized leader of the team, sensed his dominance being challenged by this unfamiliar dog from the South. Buck seemed alien to him, since among all the southern dogs he had encountered, none had proven themselves capable in camp or on the trail. They had all been too weak, perishing from the harsh labor, bitter cold, and hunger. Buck stood apart from the rest. He was the only one who survived and thrived, rivaling the husky in power, ferocity, and intelligence. Beyond that, he was a commanding dog, and what made him truly threatening was that the beating from the man in the red sweater had stripped away all his reckless courage and impulsive behavior from his drive to dominate. He had become exceptionally clever, able to wait for the right moment with a patience that was utterly primal.

It was bound to happen that the fight for leadership would come. Buck wanted it. He wanted it because it was in his nature, because he had been seized by that unnamed, mysterious pride of the trail and harness—that pride which keeps dogs working until their last breath, which draws them to die happily in their gear, and crushes their spirits if they are removed from the harness. This was the pride of Dave as the wheel-dog, of Sol-leks as he pulled with everything he had; the pride that took hold of them when camp broke, changing them from bitter and moody beasts into straining, eager, driven animals; the pride that pushed them forward all day and left them exhausted when camp was made at night, causing them to sink back into dark restlessness and dissatisfaction. This was the pride that lifted up Spitz and made him beat the sled-dogs who made mistakes and avoided work in the traces or disappeared when it was time to put on the harness in the morning. In the same way, it was this pride that made him fear Buck as a potential lead-dog. And this was Buck's pride as well.

He boldly challenged the other dog's authority as leader. He stepped in between him and the lazy dogs that deserved punishment. And he did this on purpose. One night, heavy snow fell, and when morning came, Pike, who was always trying to avoid work, was nowhere to be found. He had hidden himself safely in his den beneath a foot of snow. François called for him and searched everywhere but couldn't find him. Spitz was furious with rage. He stormed through the camp, sniffing and digging in every spot where Pike might be hiding, growling so terrifyingly that Pike could hear him and trembled in his secret hiding place.

But when he was finally dug out, and Spitz lunged at him for punishment, Buck charged forward with equal fury, positioning himself between them. The move was so unexpected and skillfully executed that Spitz was thrown backward and knocked off his feet. Pike, who had been cowering in terror, found courage in this open rebellion and attacked his fallen leader. Buck, who had long forgotten any sense of fair play, also pounced on Spitz. However, François, amused by the incident but unwavering in his duty to maintain order, brought his whip down on Buck with full force. This didn't succeed in pulling Buck away from his fallen opponent, so François used the handle of the whip as a club. Dazed by the strike, Buck was knocked backward while the lash struck him repeatedly, as Spitz thoroughly punished Pike, who had caused trouble many times before.

In the days that followed, as they drew nearer and nearer to Dawson, Buck continued to come between Spitz and the troublemakers; but he did it cleverly, when François wasn't watching. With Buck's hidden rebellion, widespread defiance broke out and grew worse. Dave and Sol-leks remained unaffected, but the rest of the team deteriorated steadily. Things stopped running smoothly. There was constant arguing and discord. Problems were always brewing, and Buck was behind all of it. He kept François on edge, since the dog-driver lived in constant fear of the life-and-death battle between the two dogs that he knew had to happen eventually; and more than once the sounds of fighting and conflict among the other dogs drove him from his sleeping bag, worried that Buck and Spitz were finally going at each other.

But the chance never came, and they arrived in Dawson one gloomy afternoon with the major confrontation still ahead of them. The town was filled with many men and countless dogs, and Buck discovered that all of them were working. It appeared to be the natural way of things that dogs should labor. Throughout the day they moved back and forth along the main street in long teams, and during the night their jingling bells continued to pass by. They transported cabin logs and firewood, carried freight up to the mines, and performed all kinds of work that horses did in the Santa Clara Valley. Occasionally Buck encountered dogs from the South, but mostly they were the wild wolf husky breed. Every night, without fail, at nine, at twelve, and at three, they raised a nighttime song, a strange and haunting chant, which Buck loved to join.

With the northern lights blazing coldly above, or the stars dancing in the freezing air, and the land lying numb and frozen beneath its blanket of snow, this howling of the huskies could have been life's defiant cry, except it was sung in a sorrowful tone, filled with drawn-out wails and muffled sobs, making it more like life's desperate plea, the voiced struggle of existence itself. This was an ancient song, as old as the breed—one of the earliest songs from the world's youth when all songs carried sadness. It carried the grief of countless generations, this mournful cry that stirred something deep and mysterious in Buck. When he whined and sobbed along, he felt the ancient pain of living that had once tormented his wild ancestors, along with the fear and wonder of cold and darkness that had filled them with the same dread and awe. The fact that this song could move him so deeply showed how completely he was reaching back through countless ages of domestication and shelter to the primitive dawn of life in those savage times.

Seven days after they arrived in Dawson, they descended the steep bank near the Barracks to reach the Yukon Trail and headed toward Dyea and Salt Water. Perrault was carrying dispatches that were even more urgent than the ones he had delivered; additionally, his competitive spirit had taken hold of him, and he intended to set the fastest travel record of the year. Several factors worked in his favor for this journey. The week of rest had restored the dogs' strength and gotten them into excellent condition. The trail they had carved through the wilderness on their way in had been packed down hard by other travelers who came after them. Furthermore, the police had established supply caches of food for both dogs and men at two or three locations along the route, allowing him to travel with a lighter load.

They reached Sixty Mile, a fifty-mile journey, on their first day, and by the second day they were racing up the Yukon River, making good progress toward Pelly. However, this excellent performance came only after considerable difficulty and frustration for François. Buck's subtle rebellion had broken apart the team's unity. The dogs no longer moved as one coordinated unit pulling together in their harnesses. Buck's support of the rebellious dogs encouraged them to commit various minor acts of defiance. Spitz was no longer a leader who commanded great respect and fear. The old reverence had vanished, and the other dogs now felt bold enough to challenge his leadership. One night, Pike stole half a fish from Spitz and devoured it while Buck protected him. On another evening, Dub and Joe attacked Spitz and forced him to abandon the discipline they had earned. Even Billee, who was naturally gentle-tempered, became less agreeable and didn't whimper as submissively as he had before. Whenever Buck approached Spitz, he would snarl and bristle threateningly. His behavior had become that of a bully, and he would strut arrogantly back and forth right in front of Spitz.

The breakdown of discipline also affected how the dogs treated each other. They fought and argued more than they ever had before, and sometimes the camp turned into a chaotic mess of howling. Only Dave and Sol-leks remained unchanged, although the constant fighting made them irritable too. François cursed with strange, crude words, stomped his feet in the snow out of helpless anger, and pulled at his hair. He constantly cracked his whip at the dogs, but it didn't help much. The moment he turned around, they started fighting again. He supported Spitz with his whip, while Buck sided with the rest of the team. François knew Buck was the cause of all the trouble, and Buck knew that François knew; but Buck was too smart to ever get caught in the act again. He worked hard and faithfully when pulling the sled, because he had grown to enjoy the work; yet he found even greater pleasure in secretly starting fights among his teammates and causing the harness lines to get tangled.

At the mouth of the Tahkeena, one evening after dinner, Dub spotted a snowshoe rabbit, lunged at it, and failed to catch it. Within seconds the entire team was chasing at full speed. A hundred yards away stood a camp belonging to the Northwest Police, housing fifty dogs, all huskies, who immediately joined the pursuit. The rabbit raced down the river, then veered off into a narrow creek, following its frozen streambed with determination. The rabbit moved effortlessly across the snow's surface, while the dogs forced their way through using sheer power. Buck led the pack of sixty dogs around curve after curve, but he couldn't close the distance. He stayed low during the chase, whimpering with excitement, his magnificent body surging forward, bound by bound, in the pale white moonlight. And bound by bound, like some ghostly frost spirit, the snowshoe rabbit continued flashing ahead.

All that awakening of ancient instincts that regularly compels people to leave the bustling cities for forests and open fields to kill animals with bullets fired by gunpowder, the thirst for blood, the pleasure of killing—all of this belonged to Buck, except it was far more personal and direct. He was leading the pack, chasing down the wild prey, the living flesh, to kill with his own fangs and cover his snout up to his eyes in warm blood.

There is a state of pure bliss that represents the highest point of existence, a peak beyond which life cannot climb any higher. This creates one of life's greatest contradictions: this overwhelming joy arrives precisely when someone feels most intensely alive, yet it manifests as complete unconsciousness of being alive at all. This profound euphoria, this total forgetting of existence itself, overwhelms the artist who becomes consumed and transported by creative fire. It seizes the soldier driven mad by battle on a devastated battlefield, refusing to surrender. And it possessed Buck as he led his pack, howling the ancient wolf call, pursuing the living prey that raced swiftly ahead of him through the pale moonlight. He was exploring the deepest layers of his being, reaching into aspects of his nature that ran deeper than his conscious self, stretching back to the very beginning of time itself. The raw surge of life completely controlled him—the overwhelming flood of pure existence, the absolute pleasure of every individual muscle, joint, and tendon celebrating that it represented everything opposite to death, that it blazed with vitality and wild energy, expressing itself through motion, soaring triumphantly beneath the stars and across the surface of lifeless matter that remained perfectly still.

But Spitz, cold and calculating even in his most intense moments, left the pack and cut across a narrow strip of land where the creek made a long curve around. Buck didn't know about this, and as he rounded the bend, the ghostly outline of a rabbit still darting before him, he saw another and larger ghostly shape leap from the overhanging bank directly into the rabbit's path. It was Spitz. The rabbit couldn't turn, and as the white teeth snapped its back in midair it screamed as loudly as any wounded man might scream. At the sound of this, the cry of Life plummeting down from Life's peak in Death's grasp, the entire pack at Buck's heels raised a hellish chorus of delight.

Buck didn't cry out. He didn't hold back, but charged straight at Spitz, shoulder to shoulder, hitting him so hard that he missed his throat. They tumbled over and over in the soft, powdery snow. Spitz got back on his feet almost as if he hadn't been knocked down at all, slashing Buck across the shoulder and jumping away. His teeth snapped together twice, like the steel jaws of a trap, as he backed up to get better footing, his thin lips curling upward as they twisted and snarled.

In an instant Buck understood. The moment had arrived. This would be a fight to the death. As they moved in circles around each other, growling, with ears flattened back, carefully watching for any opportunity, the scene struck Buck as strangely familiar. He felt like he remembered all of it—the white forest, the snowy ground, the moonlight, and the excitement of combat. A supernatural stillness hung over the white landscape and the quiet. There wasn't even the slightest breath of wind— nothing stirred, not a single leaf trembled, and the visible breath from the dogs rose slowly and hung in the freezing air. These dogs, who were barely domesticated wolves, had quickly finished off the snowshoe rabbit, and now they had formed an anticipating circle. They also remained quiet, only their eyes shining and their breath slowly drifting upward. For Buck, this ancient scene was neither new nor unusual. It felt as if it had always existed, the natural order of things.

Spitz was an experienced fighter. From Spitzbergen through the Arctic, and across Canada and the Barrens, he had maintained his dominance against all kinds of dogs and gained mastery over them. He possessed fierce anger, but it was never reckless anger. In his desire to tear apart and destroy, he never forgot that his opponent shared the same desire to tear apart and destroy. He never charged forward until he was ready to handle a charge; never launched an attack until he had first prepared his defense against that attack.

Buck fought desperately to sink his teeth into the neck of the large white dog, but his efforts were futile. Every time his fangs aimed for the tender flesh, Spitz's own fangs blocked the attack. Their teeth clashed against each other, and both dogs' lips were torn and bleeding, yet Buck couldn't break through his opponent's defenses. Buck then intensified his assault, surrounding Spitz with a flurry of rapid attacks. Again and again he lunged for the snow-white throat, where blood pulsed close to the skin, but each and every time Spitz struck back and escaped. Buck then changed tactics, pretending to charge for the throat before suddenly pulling his head back and curving around from the side, ramming his shoulder into Spitz's shoulder like a battering ram trying to knock him down. However, each attempt only resulted in Buck's shoulder being slashed as Spitz nimbly leaped out of the way.

Spitz remained unharmed, while Buck was covered in blood and breathing heavily. The battle was becoming increasingly fierce. Throughout it all, the quiet and wolf-like circle of dogs waited to destroy whichever animal fell. As Buck became exhausted, Spitz began charging at him repeatedly, keeping him struggling to maintain his balance. At one point Buck fell over, and the entire circle of sixty dogs rose up; however, he regained his footing, almost while still in the air, and the circle settled back down and continued waiting.

But Buck had a quality that made him truly great—imagination. He fought using instinct, but he could also fight using strategy. He charged forward, as if he was going to use the old shoulder move, but at the last moment he dropped low to the snow and lunged in. His teeth clamped down on Spitz's left front leg. There was a sharp crack of bone breaking, and the white dog now faced him standing on only three legs. Three times Buck tried to knock him down, then he used the same trick again and broke Spitz's right front leg. Even though he was in pain and helpless, Spitz fought desperately to stay on his feet. He could see the silent circle of dogs, with their bright eyes, hanging tongues, and silvery breath rising in the air, moving closer to him just as he had watched similar circles close in on defeated opponents before. But this time, he was the one who had been defeated.

There was no hope for him. Buck was relentless. Mercy was something meant for kinder places. He positioned himself for the final attack. The circle had closed in until he could feel the huskies breathing on his sides. He could see them, beyond Spitz and on both sides, crouching low and ready to leap, their eyes locked on him. A moment of stillness seemed to settle over everything. Every animal froze as if turned to stone. Only Spitz trembled and bristled as he stumbled back and forth, growling with terrifying threat, as if trying to scare away approaching death. Then Buck lunged forward and back; but while he was moving in, shoulder had finally met shoulder squarely. The dark circle shrank to a small spot on the moonlit snow as Spitz vanished from sight. Buck stood watching, the victorious champion, the ruling primitive beast who had made his kill and found it satisfying.

Chapter IV:
Who Has Achieved Mastery

"What? What did I say? I spoke the truth when I said that Buck was two devils." This was what François said the next morning when he discovered Spitz was missing and Buck was covered with wounds. He brought him to the fire and by its light pointed them out.

"That Spitz fights like hell," said Perrault, as he examined the gaping tears and wounds.

"And that Buck fights like two hells," was François's answer. "And now we make good time. No more Spitz, no more trouble, sure."

While Perrault packed the camping gear and loaded the sled, the dog driver began harnessing the dogs. Buck trotted over to the spot where Spitz would have stood as the lead dog, but François didn't notice him and brought Sol-leks to the desired position instead. In his opinion, Sol-leks was the best remaining lead dog. Buck lunged at Sol-leks in a rage, forcing him back and taking his place.

"What? What?" François shouted, slapping his thighs with delight. "Look at that Buck. He killed that Spitz, and now he thinks he's going to take over the job."

"Get away, Chook!" he shouted, but Buck wouldn't move.

He grabbed Buck by the scruff of his neck, and even though the dog growled menacingly, he pulled him aside and put Sol-leks back in his place. The older dog clearly didn't like this arrangement and made it obvious that he was scared of Buck. François remained stubborn about his decision, but the moment he turned around, Buck pushed Sol-leks out of position again, and Sol-leks was more than happy to step aside.

François was furious. "Now, by God, I'll fix you!" he shouted, returning with a heavy club in his hand.

Buck remembered the man in the red sweater and slowly backed away; he didn't try to rush forward when Sol-leks was brought up again. Instead, he circled just outside the reach of the club, growling with anger and fury; as he moved in circles, he kept his eyes on the club, ready to dodge if François decided to throw it, since he had learned how clubs worked. The driver continued with his task and called to Buck when he was ready to put him back in his usual spot in front of Dave. Buck took two or three steps backward. François moved toward him, which made Buck retreat again. After this went on for a while, François dropped the club, thinking that Buck was afraid of getting beaten. But Buck was in complete rebellion. He didn't want to avoid a beating—he wanted to be the leader. The position belonged to him by right. He had worked for it, and he wouldn't settle for anything less.

Perrault joined in. Together they chased him around for most of an hour. They hurled sticks at him. He dodged them. They swore at him, cursing his ancestors and descendants down to the most distant generation, and every hair on his body and drop of blood in his veins; and he responded to their curses with growls while staying beyond their reach. He made no attempt to flee, but instead circled around and around the camp, making it clear that once his needs were satisfied, he would return and behave.

François sat down and scratched his head. Perrault glanced at his watch and cursed. Time was slipping away, and they should have been on the trail an hour ago. François scratched his head once more. He shook it and smiled awkwardly at the courier, who shrugged his shoulders to show they had been defeated. Then François walked over to where Sol-leks was standing and called out to Buck. Buck laughed the way dogs laugh, but still kept his distance. François unhooked Sol-leks's harness and returned him to his former position. The team stood hitched to the sled in a continuous line, prepared for the trail. There was no spot for Buck except at the front. Again François called out, and again Buck laughed and stayed away.

"Throw down the club," Perrault commanded.

François agreed, and Buck trotted in with a triumphant laugh, swinging around to take his position at the front of the team. His harness was secured, the sled was freed from the snow, and with both men running alongside, they raced out onto the river trail.

Even though the dog-driver had placed a high value on Buck and his two companions, he discovered before the day was over that he had actually underestimated them. Buck immediately took charge as the leader, and when situations demanded good judgment, fast thinking, and quick action, he proved himself superior even to Spitz, whom François had never seen matched by any other dog.

But Buck truly shined when it came to establishing rules and ensuring his teammates followed them. Dave and Sol-leks weren't bothered by the change in leadership. It wasn't their concern. Their job was to work hard, pulling with all their strength in the harnesses. As long as no one interfered with that, they didn't care what else went on. For all they cared, even Billee, with his easygoing nature, could have been the leader, provided he maintained order. The other dogs on the team, however, had become difficult to manage during Spitz's final days, and they were shocked when Buck began whipping them into line.

Pike, who nipped at Buck's heels and never put any more effort into pulling against the harness than absolutely necessary, was quickly and repeatedly disciplined for slacking off; and before the first day ended he was working harder than he ever had in his life. That first night at camp, Joe, the bad-tempered one, received a thorough beating— something that Spitz had never managed to accomplish. Buck simply overpowered him with his superior weight, and tore into him until he stopped snarling and started whimpering for mercy.

The team's overall spirit improved right away. The group regained its former unity, and once again the dogs moved together as one in their harnesses. At the Rink Rapids, two local huskies named Teek and Koona joined the team, and the speed with which Buck trained them left François amazed.

"Never such a dog as that Buck!" he cried. "No, never! He's worth one thousand dollars, by God! Eh? What do you say, Perrault?"

Perrault nodded in agreement. He was beating the previous record at that point, and his lead was growing with each passing day. The trail conditions were perfect, firmly packed and solid, with no fresh snowfall to slow them down. The weather wasn't unbearably cold. The temperature fell to fifty degrees below zero and stayed at that level throughout their entire journey. The men alternated between riding and running, while the dogs maintained a steady pace with only occasional brief stops.

The Thirty Mile River was relatively covered with ice, and they completed in one day going out what had taken them ten days coming in. In a single run they made a sixty-mile dash from the foot of Lake Le Barge to the White Horse Rapids. Across Marsh, Tagish, and Bennett (seventy miles of lakes), they flew so fast that the man whose turn it was to run was towed behind the sled at the end of a rope. And on the last night of the second week they reached the top of White Pass and descended down the sea slope with the lights of Skaguay and of the ships at their feet.

It was a record-breaking journey. Every day for two weeks they had covered an average of forty miles. For three days Perrault and François strutted up and down Skaguay's main street and were flooded with offers to buy them drinks, while their dog team remained the focus of an admiring crowd of dog drivers and sledders. Then three or four western outlaws tried to take over the town, got shot full of holes for their trouble, and the public's attention shifted to new heroes. Then the official orders arrived. François called Buck over to him, wrapped his arms around him, and cried over him. That was the last Buck ever saw of François and Perrault. Like other people, they disappeared from Buck's life forever.

A Scottish mixed-race man took control of him and his fellow dogs, and together with a dozen other dog teams, he began the long journey back along the exhausting trail to Dawson. This wasn't easy running anymore, nor was it about breaking records, but rather grueling work every day with a heavy load to pull behind them; this was the mail train, delivering messages from the outside world to the men who searched for gold in the remote northern wilderness.

Buck didn't enjoy it, but he handled the work well, developing a sense of pride in it similar to Dave and Sol-leks, and making sure that his teammates did their part, whether they took pride in it or not. The routine was repetitive, running with clockwork precision. Each day resembled the next. Every morning at the same time, the cooks got up, built fires, and prepared breakfast. Afterward, while some people packed up camp, others got the dogs ready with their harnesses, and the team would be moving within an hour or so before the darkness that signaled the approaching dawn. When evening came, they set up camp. Some put up the tents, others gathered firewood and pine branches for bedding, while still others fetched water or ice for the cooks. The dogs also received their meals. For them, this feeding time was the highlight of each day, although it felt good to relax afterward for an hour or so with the other dogs once they had finished eating their fish—there were about a hundred and twenty dogs in total. Some of them were aggressive fighters, but after three fights with the most violent ones, Buck established his dominance, so that whenever he showed aggression and bared his teeth, the others would move away from him.

Best of all, perhaps, he loved to lie near the fire, hind legs tucked beneath him, front legs extended ahead, head lifted, and eyes gazing drowsily at the flames. Sometimes he thought of Judge Miller's large house in the sunny Santa Clara Valley, and of the concrete swimming pool, and Ysabel, the Mexican hairless dog, and Toots, the Japanese pug; but more often he recalled the man in the red sweater, the death of Curly, the fierce battle with Spitz, and the good food he had eaten or wanted to eat. He wasn't homesick. The Sunland seemed very faint and far away, and those memories held no influence over him. Much stronger were the memories from his ancestry that made things he had never seen before feel strangely familiar; the instincts (which were simply the memories of his forebears turned into habits) that had faded in recent generations, and even later, in him, stirred and came alive once more.

Sometimes as he crouched there, blinking sleepily at the flames, it felt like the fire belonged to another time, and that as he sat by this different fire he could see another man entirely—not the mixed-race cook sitting before him. This other man had shorter legs and longer arms, with muscles that were lean and gnarled rather than smooth and bulging. This man's hair was long and tangled, and his head tilted backward beneath it, sloping away from his eyes. He made strange noises and appeared terrified of the darkness, constantly staring into it while gripping a stick in his hand—which hung halfway between his knee and foot—with a heavy stone tied to one end. He wore almost nothing, just a torn and fire-damaged animal skin that partially covered his back, but his body was covered with thick hair. In certain areas, across his chest and shoulders and down the outer parts of his arms and legs, the hair had grown so thick it was almost like fur. He didn't stand upright, but leaned forward from his waist on legs that were bent at the knees. His whole body had an unusual flexibility and bounce to it, almost like a cat, along with the quick awareness of someone who lived in constant fear of both visible and invisible threats.

At other times this hairy man crouched by the fire with his head between his legs and slept. During these moments his elbows rested on his knees, his hands clasped above his head as if to deflect rain with his hairy arms. And beyond that fire, in the surrounding darkness, Buck could see many glowing coals, two by two, always two by two, which he knew to be the eyes of great predatory beasts. And he could hear the crashing of their bodies through the underbrush, and the sounds they made in the night. And dreaming there by the Yukon bank, with drowsy eyes blinking at the fire, these sounds and sights of another world would make the hair rise along his back and stand on end across his shoulders and up his neck, until he whimpered quietly and restrainedly, or growled softly, and the half-breed cook yelled at him, "Hey, you Buck, wake up!" At which point the other world would disappear and the real world would come into his eyes, and he would get up and yawn and stretch as if he had been asleep.

It was a difficult journey, with the mail weighing them down, and the demanding work exhausted them. They were underweight and in poor shape when they reached Dawson, and they should have rested for at least a week or ten days. However, within two days they descended the Yukon bank from the Barracks, carrying letters bound for the outside world. The dogs were exhausted, the drivers were complaining, and to make things worse, it snowed daily. This created a soft trail, increased friction on the sled runners, and made pulling much harder for the dogs; nevertheless, the drivers remained fair throughout it all, and they did everything they could for the animals.

Every evening, the dogs received care before anyone else. The dogs were fed before their handlers had their own meals, and no driver would reach for his bedroll until he had thoroughly checked the paws of each dog in his team. Even so, their stamina continued to decline. From the start of winter, they had covered eighteen hundred miles, pulling sleds across every exhausting mile of that journey; such a distance takes its toll on even the strongest creatures. Buck endured it all, pushing his teammates to keep working and upholding order within the pack, though he too felt deeply exhausted. Each night, Billee would cry and whine in his sleep without fail. Joe had grown more bitter than before, and Sol-leks remained impossible to approach, whether from his blind side or his good side.

But it was Dave who suffered the most. Something had gone wrong with him. He grew increasingly gloomy and bad-tempered, and whenever they set up camp, he immediately made his bed where his driver would feed him. Once he was freed from his harness and lay down, he wouldn't stand up again until it was time to be harnessed the next morning. Sometimes, while pulling in the traces, when the sled suddenly stopped or when he strained to get it moving, he would cry out in pain. The driver checked him over but couldn't find anything wrong. All the drivers became concerned about his condition. They discussed it during meals and while smoking their final pipes before turning in for the night, and one evening they gathered for a thorough examination. They brought him from his resting place to the fire and pressed and poked him until he yelped repeatedly. Something was definitely wrong internally, but they couldn't locate any broken bones and couldn't figure out what it was.

By the time they reached Cassiar Bar, Dave had become so weak that he kept falling down while pulling the sled. The Scottish half-breed stopped the team and removed Dave from his position, putting Sol-leks, the next dog in line, in his place to pull the sled. He planned to let Dave rest by allowing him to run freely behind the sled. Even though Dave was sick, he hated being taken out of the harness, making grumbling and growling sounds as they unfastened the straps, and whining pitifully when he saw Sol-leks taking over the position he had occupied and worked in for so long. Dave took great pride in being part of the team and working the trail, and even though he was dying, he couldn't stand the thought of another dog doing his job.

When the sled began moving, he struggled through the deep snow beside the packed trail, biting at Sol-leks with his teeth, charging into him and attempting to push him off into the soft snow on the opposite side, trying to jump inside his harness and position himself between Sol-leks and the sled, all while whimpering and barking and crying out in sorrow and agony. The mixed-blood driver attempted to chase him away with the whip, but he ignored the sharp sting of the lash, and the man couldn't bring himself to strike any harder. Dave wouldn't run calmly on the trail behind the sled, where travel was simple, but kept struggling alongside in the deep snow, where movement was extremely hard, until he was completely worn out. Finally he collapsed, and remained where he had fallen, wailing mournfully as the long line of sleds passed him by.

Using the last bit of strength he had left, he managed to stumble along behind the other sleds until the train stopped again. When it did, he struggled past the other sleds to reach his own, where he positioned himself next to Sol-leks. His driver paused briefly to light his pipe using a flame from another musher. After that, he came back and gave the command for his dogs to move. The team started forward on the trail with surprising ease, but then they turned their heads nervously and came to an unexpected halt. The driver was just as confused as his dogs—the sled hadn't budged an inch. He called out to the other mushers to come see what was happening. Dave had chewed completely through both of Sol-leks's harness straps and was now standing directly in front of the sled, right where he belonged.

He begged with his eyes to stay where he was. The driver felt confused and uncertain. His fellow workers discussed how a dog could have its heart broken by being prevented from doing the work that was destroying it, and they remembered cases they had witnessed where dogs that were too old for the hard labor, or hurt, had died simply because they were removed from their harnesses. They also believed it would be a kindness, since Dave was going to die regardless, for him to die while still pulling the sled, feeling peaceful and satisfied. So they put him back in his harness, and he pulled with the same pride as before, even though he couldn't help crying out several times from the sharp pain inside him. He collapsed multiple times and was pulled along in his harness, and at one point the sled rolled over him, leaving him with a permanent limp in one of his back legs.

But he managed to hold on until they reached camp, where his driver created a spot for him near the fire. When morning came, he was too weak to continue the journey. At the time when the team was being harnessed, he attempted to crawl toward his driver. Through spasmodic struggles, he managed to get to his feet, wobbled unsteadily, and collapsed. Then he slowly dragged himself forward toward the place where his teammates were being fitted with their harnesses. He would push his front legs ahead and pull his body along with a jerky, lurching motion, then extend his front legs again and drag himself forward another few inches. His energy gave out, and the final image his teammates had of him was lying in the snow, breathing heavily and gazing longingly in their direction. However, they could still hear his sorrowful howling until they disappeared from view beyond a line of trees along the riverbank.

Here the train came to a stop. The Scottish mixed-race man slowly walked back to the camp they had abandoned. The men stopped talking. A gunshot echoed through the air. The man returned quickly. The whips cracked, the bells jingled cheerfully, the sleds moved along the path; but Buck understood, and every dog understood, what had happened behind the line of trees along the river.

Chapter V:
The Toil of Trace and Trail

Thirty days after leaving Dawson, the Salt Water Mail arrived at Skaguay with Buck and his teammates pulling at the front. They were in terrible condition, exhausted and completely worn down. Buck's weight had dropped from one hundred and forty pounds to just one hundred and fifteen. His teammates, although they were smaller dogs, had lost even more weight proportionally than he had. Pike, who was known for faking injuries and had spent his whole life being dishonest, often pretending to have a hurt leg, was now genuinely limping. Sol-leks was also limping, and Dub was dealing with a pulled shoulder blade.

They were all extremely sore on their feet. No energy or bounce remained in them. Their feet hit the trail hard, shaking their bodies and making each day's journey twice as exhausting. Nothing was wrong with them other than complete exhaustion. This wasn't the kind of bone-deep tiredness that comes from short bursts of intense effort, where you can recover in just a few hours; instead, it was the kind of exhaustion that develops from months of steady, draining work that slowly saps your strength. They had no ability to bounce back left, no backup energy to draw from. Everything had been used up, down to the very last bit. Every muscle, every fiber, every cell was tired—completely worn out. And there was good reason for this condition. In under five months, they had covered twenty-five hundred miles, and during the final eighteen hundred miles of that distance, they had rested for only five days. When they reached Skaguay, they were clearly at the end of their rope. They could barely keep the harness straps tight, and going downhill they just barely managed to stay ahead of the sled.

"Keep going, you poor sore feet," the driver encouraged them as they stumbled down the main street of Skagway. "This is the last one. Then we get a long rest. Right? For sure. One really long rest."

The drivers fully expected to have a long break. They had traveled twelve hundred miles with only two days of rest, and by any reasonable standard of fairness, they deserved some time to relax. However, so many men had rushed into the Klondike, and so many sweethearts, wives, and relatives had stayed behind, that the backed-up mail was reaching enormous proportions; additionally, there were official orders to follow. New groups of Hudson Bay dogs were going to replace those that were no longer fit for the trail. The unfit ones needed to be removed, and since dogs matter little when money is involved, they were going to be sold.

Three days went by, and during this time Buck and his companions discovered just how exhausted and weakened they had become. Then, on the morning of the fourth day, two men from the United States arrived and purchased them, complete with harness, for practically nothing. The men called each other "Hal" and "Charles." Charles was a middle-aged man with pale coloring, featuring weak and watery eyes and a mustache that curled upward with fierce energy, contradicting the weak, drooping lip it hid beneath. Hal was a young man of nineteen or twenty, wearing a large

Colt revolver and a hunting knife attached to a belt that was packed with ammunition cartridges. This belt was his most noticeable feature. It revealed his inexperience—an inexperience that was complete and beyond description. Both men were clearly out of their element, and why people like them would venture into the North remains one of those mysterious things that defies explanation.

Buck heard the bargaining, watched the money change hands between the man and the Government agent, and understood that the Scottish half-breed and the mail-train drivers were leaving his life just as Perrault and François and the others had done before them. When he was taken with his teammates to the new owners' camp, Buck observed a careless and messy operation, with the tent only partially set up, dirty dishes left unwashed, and everything in complete disarray; he also noticed a woman there. The men referred to her as "Mercedes." She was Charles's wife and Hal's sister—quite the family gathering.

Buck watched them nervously as they began dismantling the tent and packing the sled. They put considerable effort into their work, but lacked any organized approach. They rolled the tent into a clumsy bundle that was three times larger than necessary. They packed away the tin dishes without washing them. Mercedes constantly got in her companions' way while maintaining a steady stream of complaints and suggestions. When they placed a clothes bag at the front of the sled, she insisted it belonged in the back; after they moved it to the back and covered it with several other bundles, she remembered forgotten items that could only fit in that particular bag, forcing them to unpack everything once more.

Three men emerged from a nearby tent and stood watching, smiling and exchanging knowing glances with each other.

"You already have quite a heavy load," said one of them; "and it's not my place to tell you what to do, but I wouldn't carry that tent with me if I were you."

"Unthinkable!" Mercedes exclaimed, raising her hands in delicate horror. "How on earth could I possibly survive without a tent?"

"It's springtime, and you won't get any more cold weather," the man replied.

She shook her head firmly, and Charles and Hal placed the final miscellaneous items on top of the enormous pile of cargo.

"Think it'll ride?" one of the men asked.

"Why shouldn't it?" Charles asked somewhat curtly.

"Oh, that's perfectly fine, that's perfectly fine," the man quickly said in a humble tone. "I was just wondering, that's all. It just seemed a bit top-heavy to me."

Charles turned around and pulled the ropes down as best he could manage, though his efforts were far from adequate.

"And of course the dogs can walk all day with that device behind them," confirmed another one of the men.

"Absolutely," Hal replied with icy courtesy, gripping the steering pole with one hand while brandishing his whip with the other. "Mush!" he yelled. "Get moving!"

The dogs lunged forward against their harnesses, pulling with all their strength for several moments before giving up. They couldn't budge the sled.

"Those lazy animals, I'll teach them a lesson," he shouted, getting ready to strike them with the whip.

But Mercedes stepped in, crying out, "Oh, Hal, you can't do that!" as she grabbed the whip and pulled it away from him. "Those poor animals! You have to promise me you won't treat them badly for the rest of our journey, or I'm not taking another step."

"You don't know much about dogs," her brother sneered; "and I wish you'd leave me alone. They're lazy, I tell you, and you have to whip them to get anything out of them. That's just how they are. You can ask anyone. Ask one of those men."

Mercedes looked at them with pleading eyes, her beautiful face showing clear disgust at witnessing such suffering.

"They're completely exhausted, if you want to know," came the reply from one of the men. "Completely worn out, that's what's wrong with them. They need a rest."

"Forget about rest," said Hal, with his smooth, young lips; and Mercedes said, "Oh!" in pain and sorrow at his harsh words.

"But she was a clannish creature, and rushed at once to the defence of her brother. "Never mind that man," she said pointedly. "You're driving our dogs, and you do what you think best with them.""

Once more Hal's whip struck the dogs. They pressed themselves against the harnesses, planted their feet firmly in the hard-packed snow, crouched low, and exerted every ounce of their strength. The sled remained motionless as if it were anchored in place. After two attempts, they stopped and stood gasping for breath. The whip was cutting through the air viciously when Mercedes stepped in again. She fell to her knees in front of Buck, tears streaming down her face, and wrapped her arms around his neck.

"You poor, poor things," she called out with sympathy, "why don't you pull harder?—then you wouldn't get whipped." Buck didn't like her, but he felt too wretched to fight back, accepting it as just another part of the day's awful work.

One of the bystanders, who had been gritting his teeth to hold back angry words, finally spoke up:

"I don't care one bit what happens to you, but for the sake of the dogs I need to tell you something—you can help them tremendously by freeing that sled. The runners are frozen solid. Put your full weight against the steering pole, pushing right and left, and break it loose."

A third time they made the attempt, but this time, following the advice, Hal broke out the runners that had frozen to the snow. The overloaded and unwieldy sled pushed forward, Buck and his teammates struggling desperately under the shower of blows. A hundred yards ahead the path turned and sloped steeply into the main street. It would have taken an experienced man to keep the top-heavy sled upright, and Hal was not such a man. As they swung around the turn the sled tipped over, spilling half its load through the loose bindings. The dogs never stopped. The lightened sled bounced on its side behind them. They were furious because of the poor treatment they had received and the unfair load. Buck was enraged. He broke into a run, the team following his lead. Hal shouted "Whoa! whoa!" but they paid no attention. He stumbled and was pulled off his feet. The overturned sled scraped over him, and the dogs raced on up the street, adding to the excitement of Skaguay as they scattered the rest of the supplies along its main thoroughfare.

Kind-hearted citizens caught the dogs and gathered up the scattered belongings. They also offered advice. If they ever expected to reach Dawson, they needed half the load and twice as many dogs—that's what people told them. Hal and his sister and brother-in-law listened reluctantly, set up their tent, and went through their supplies. They unpacked canned goods that made men laugh, because canned goods on the Long Trail were something you could only dream about. "Blankets for a hotel," said one of the men who laughed while helping them. "Even half that many is too much; get rid of them. Throw away that tent and all those dishes—who's going to wash them anyway? Good Lord, do you think you're traveling on a luxury train?"

And so it continued, the relentless removal of everything unnecessary. Mercedes wept when her clothing bags were thrown onto the ground and item after item was tossed aside. She cried constantly, and she cried specifically over each rejected item. She wrapped her arms around her knees, rocking back and forth in heartbreak. She declared she wouldn't move a single step, not even for a dozen men like Charles. She pleaded with everyone and everything around her, eventually drying her tears and beginning to throw out even pieces of clothing that were absolutely essential. And in her enthusiasm, once she had finished with her own belongings, she turned on her companions' possessions and tore through them like a whirlwind.

Once this was done, the supplies, even though reduced by half, still formed an enormous load. Charles and Hal headed out that evening and purchased six dogs from the Outside. These new dogs, combined with the six from the original team plus Teek and Koona—the huskies they had acquired at the Rink Rapids during the record journey—brought their total team to fourteen dogs. However, the Outside dogs, despite being somewhat trained since they arrived, weren't worth much. Three of them were short-haired pointers, one was a Newfoundland, and the remaining two were mixed breeds of uncertain ancestry. These newcomers seemed completely clueless. Buck and his teammates viewed them with contempt, and while he quickly showed them their position in the pack and what they shouldn't do, he couldn't teach them what they should do. They struggled to adapt to the harness and the trail. Except for the two mixed breeds, the others were confused and demoralized by the harsh, unfamiliar wilderness they now faced and the rough treatment they had endured. The two mixed breeds had no fight left in them whatsoever; their bones were the only solid things about them.

With the new dogs feeling hopeless and dejected, and the experienced team exhausted from twenty-five hundred miles of nonstop travel, the situation looked far from promising. The two men, though, remained quite upbeat. They felt proud as well. They were handling this journey in grand fashion, with fourteen dogs. They had watched other sleds leave over the Pass heading to Dawson, or arrive from Dawson, but they had never witnessed a sled pulled by as many as fourteen dogs. In Arctic travel, there was a practical reason why fourteen dogs shouldn't pull a single sled, and that reason was that one sled couldn't transport enough food to feed fourteen dogs. But Charles and Hal were unaware of this fact. They had calculated the trip using pencil and paper, determining so much food per dog, so many dogs, so many days, Q.E.D. Mercedes peered over their shoulders and nodded with understanding, since it all seemed so straightforward.

The following morning, Buck led the long team of dogs up the street. There was no energy or enthusiasm in him or his companions. They were beginning the journey completely exhausted. He had already traveled the route between Salt Water and Dawson four times, and knowing that he was worn out and weary yet had to face the same trail again filled him with resentment. His heart wasn't in the work, and neither was any other dog's. The outside dogs were nervous and scared, while the inside dogs had lost faith in their masters.

Buck sensed instinctively that these two men and the woman couldn't be trusted. They were completely incompetent, and as time passed, it became clear they were incapable of learning anything. They approached everything carelessly, lacking any sense of organization or self-control. Setting up their messy camp consumed half the night, and breaking it down the next morning took half the day, with the sled packed so haphazardly that they spent the remainder of each day constantly stopping to reorganize their cargo. Some days they barely covered ten miles. Other days they couldn't even manage to get moving at all. Not once did they achieve even half the daily distance that the men had used as the foundation for calculating their dog food supplies.

It was bound to happen that they would run out of dog food. However, they sped up this process by giving the dogs too much food, which brought them closer to the day when there wouldn't be enough to feed them properly. The dogs from outside weren't used to going hungry like the sled dogs were, so they had huge appetites and wanted to eat constantly. When the exhausted huskies could barely pull the sled, Hal thought the normal amount of food wasn't enough. He gave them twice as much. To make matters worse, when Mercedes looked at him with tears in her beautiful eyes and a shaky voice, trying to convince him to feed the dogs even more, and he refused, she secretly took fish from the supply bags and fed them when no one was looking. What Buck and the other huskies really needed wasn't more food, though—it was rest. Even though they weren't covering much distance each day, the heavy load they had to drag was draining their energy completely.

Then came the period of underfeeding. Hal woke up one morning to realize that his dog food supply was half depleted while they had only covered a quarter of their journey; moreover, no additional dog food could be purchased at any price. Therefore, he reduced even the standard rations and attempted to extend their daily travel distance. His sister and brother-in-law supported his decision; however, they were hindered by their excessive equipment and their own lack of skill. While it was straightforward to reduce the dogs' food portions, it proved impossible to make the dogs move faster, and their own inability to break camp earlier each morning prevented them from traveling for longer periods. They not only lacked knowledge about handling dogs, but they also didn't understand how to manage themselves effectively.

The first to die was Dub. He was a poor, clumsy thief who constantly got caught and punished, but he had always been a reliable worker. His injured shoulder blade, left untreated and without rest, continued to deteriorate until Hal finally shot him with the large Colt revolver. There's a local saying that an Outside dog will starve to death on a husky's food ration, so the six Outside dogs working under Buck could only expect to die on half a husky's ration. The Newfoundland died first, then the three short-haired pointers, while the two mixed breeds clung to life more stubbornly before eventually succumbing as well.

By this time, all the comforts and refined manners of the South had disappeared from the three travelers. Stripped of its allure and adventure, Arctic travel became a reality too brutal for them to handle. Mercedes stopped crying over the dogs, being too busy crying over herself and fighting with her husband and brother. Fighting was the one thing they never felt too exhausted to do. Their irritation grew from their suffering, intensified with it, multiplied because of it, and eventually surpassed it. The remarkable endurance that comes to those who work hard and endure great pain while remaining gentle in their words and kind in their actions never came to these two men and the woman. They had no understanding of such endurance. They were stiff and hurting; their muscles were sore, their bones ached, their very hearts were in pain; and because of this suffering they became harsh in their speech, with cruel words being the first thing on their lips each morning and the last thing at night.

Charles and Hal argued constantly whenever Mercedes gave them the opportunity. Each man firmly believed he was doing more than his fair share of the work, and both made sure to voice this conviction at every chance they got. Sometimes Mercedes took her husband's side, other times she supported her brother. The outcome was an ongoing and bitter family feud. What might begin as a simple disagreement about who should gather some wood for the fire (a dispute that initially involved only Charles and Hal) would soon drag in the entire extended family—fathers, mothers, uncles, cousins, relatives living thousands of miles away, and even some who had passed away. How Hal's opinions about art, or the type of society plays his mother's brother had written, could possibly relate to chopping firewood was beyond understanding; yet the argument was just as likely to head in that direction as it was to focus on Charles's political biases. And how Charles's sister's gossiping habits could have any bearing on building a fire in the Yukon was clear only to Mercedes, who freely shared her extensive thoughts on that subject, along with her views on several other unpleasant characteristics she attributed to her husband's relatives. Meanwhile, the fire stayed unlit, the camp remained only partially set up, and the dogs went hungry.

Mercedes harbored a particular resentment—the resentment of her gender. She was attractive and delicate, and had received courteous treatment throughout her life. However, the current treatment from her husband and brother was anything but courteous. She was accustomed to being helpless. They grumbled about this. When they criticized what she considered her most fundamental feminine privilege, she made their lives unbearable. She no longer gave any thought to the dogs, and because she was aching and exhausted, she insisted on riding on the sled. She was attractive and delicate, but she weighed one hundred and twenty pounds—a substantial final burden added to the load pulled by the weak and starving animals. She rode for days, until they collapsed in their harnesses and the sled came to a halt. Charles and Hal begged her to get off and walk, pleaded with her, implored her, while she cried and called upon Heaven with an account of their cruelty.

On one occasion, they forcibly removed her from the sled using sheer strength. They never attempted this again. She allowed her legs to go completely limp like a petulant child and simply sat down right on the trail. They continued on their journey, but she refused to budge. After they had traveled three miles, they unloaded the sled, returned for her, and once again used brute force to place her back on the sled.

In their overwhelming misery, they became indifferent to their animals' suffering. Hal believed in a theory he imposed on others: that people must become tough and unfeeling. He had begun by preaching this philosophy to his sister and brother-in-law. When that failed, he beat the lesson into the dogs with a club. At Five Fingers, their dog food ran out, and a toothless old Native woman offered to exchange a few pounds of frozen horse hide for the Colt revolver that hung alongside the large hunting knife at Hal's hip. This hide made a terrible substitute for food, having been stripped from starving horses belonging to cattlemen six months earlier. In its frozen condition, it resembled strips of galvanized metal, and when a dog managed to force it down, the hide thawed in their stomachs into thin, worthless leather strands mixed with clumps of short hair that were both irritating and impossible to digest.

Throughout this ordeal, Buck stumbled forward at the front of the team like he was trapped in a terrible dream. He pulled the sled when his strength allowed; when he couldn't pull anymore, he collapsed and stayed down until the sting of the whip or the blow of a club forced him back to his feet. His once-magnificent coat had lost all its shine and thickness. His fur now hung limp and matted, stained with dried blood from where Hal's club had struck him. His muscles had shrunk to stringy knots, and the fat pads had vanished completely, leaving every rib and bone clearly visible beneath loose skin that hung in empty folds. The sight was heartbreaking, but Buck's spirit remained unbroken. The man in the red sweater had proven that much.

Just like Buck, his companions were in the same terrible condition. They had become walking skeletons. There were seven dogs in total, including Buck himself. Their suffering had grown so intense that they could no longer feel the sting of the whip or the impact of the club. The pain from the beatings felt numb and far away, just like everything they saw with their eyes and heard with their ears seemed muted and distant. They weren't half alive, or even a quarter alive. They were nothing more than collections of bones held together by barely flickering sparks of life. Whenever they stopped to rest, they collapsed in their harnesses like lifeless dogs, and that tiny spark of life grew dim and pale, appearing ready to die out completely. When the club or whip struck them, the spark would weakly flicker back to life, and they would struggle to stand up and stumble forward once more.

There came a day when Billee, the good-natured dog, collapsed and couldn't get back up. Since Hal had traded away his revolver, he grabbed the axe and struck Billee in the head while he lay in the harness, then cut the body free from the gear and pulled it aside. Buck witnessed this, as did his teammates, and they all understood that this fate was drawing very near to them as well. The following day, Koona died, leaving only five of them alive: Joe, who was too weak to be aggressive anymore; Pike, who was injured and limping, barely conscious and no longer alert enough to fake illness; Sol-leks, the one-eyed dog, who remained dedicated to the hard work of pulling the sled along the trail, though he was sad because he had so little energy left to contribute; Teek, who hadn't traveled as far that winter and was now being beaten more severely than the others because he still had some strength left; and Buck, who continued to lead the team but no longer tried to maintain order or discipline, often blinded by exhaustion and finding his way along the trail only by its shadowy outline and the faint sensation under his paws.

It was gorgeous spring weather, though neither the dogs nor the people paid any attention to it. Every day the sun came up earlier and went down later. Dawn broke at three in the morning, and dusk didn't fade until nine at night. The entire long day blazed with sunlight. The eerie winter quiet had been replaced by the magnificent spring chorus of life awakening. This chorus rose from everywhere across the land, filled with the happiness of being alive. It emerged from all the creatures that lived and moved once more, creatures that had seemed dead and motionless throughout the long frozen months. Sap flowed upward through the pine trees. The willows and aspens burst forth with fresh young buds. Bushes and vines dressed themselves in new green clothing. Crickets chirped through the nights, and during the days all kinds of creeping, crawling creatures rustled out into the sunlight. Partridges and woodpeckers drummed and tapped throughout the forest. Squirrels chattered, birds sang their songs, and high above honked the wild birds flying north from the south in clever V-formations that cut through the air.

From every hillside came the sound of flowing water, the melody of hidden springs. Everything was melting, bending, and breaking apart. The Yukon River was struggling to break free from the ice that held it captive. The current eroded it from below while the sun melted it from above. Breathing holes appeared, cracks formed and widened, and thin pieces of ice broke off completely and fell into the river. And in the middle of all this bursting, tearing, and pulsing of life returning, beneath the brilliant sun and through the gentle whispers of wind, the two men, the woman, and the huskies stumbled forward like travelers heading toward death.

With the dogs collapsing, Mercedes crying and riding, Hal cursing harmlessly, and Charles's eyes tearfully watering, they stumbled into John Thornton's camp at the mouth of

White River. When they stopped, the dogs fell to the ground as if they had all been struck dead. Mercedes wiped her eyes and looked at John Thornton. Charles sat down on a log to rest. He lowered himself very slowly and carefully because of his severe stiffness. Hal did the talking. John Thornton was carving the finishing touches on an axe handle he had crafted from a piece of birch wood. He carved and listened, offered brief responses, and when asked, gave short advice. He understood their type, and he shared his guidance knowing with certainty that it wouldn't be heeded.

"The people up ahead warned us that the trail was completely falling apart and that our best option was to stop and wait," Hal said in response to Thornton's warning not to take any more risks on the deteriorating ice. "They said we'd never make it to White River, and yet here we are." He spoke these final words with a mocking tone of victory.

"And they were telling you the truth," John Thornton replied. "The bottom could give way at any second. Only fools, with the kind of blind luck that fools have, could have made it across. I'm telling you straight up, I wouldn't risk my life on that ice for all the gold in Alaska."

"That's because you're not a fool, I suppose," Hal said. "All the same, we'll go on to Dawson." He uncoiled his whip. "Get up there, Buck! Hi! Get up there! Mush on!"

Thornton continued whittling. He understood it was pointless to interfere when someone was determined to act foolishly; whether there were two or three more fools in the world wouldn't change anything in the grand scheme of things.

But the team didn't stand up when ordered. They had reached the point where beatings were necessary to get them moving. The whip cracked through the air, striking without mercy wherever it landed. John Thornton pressed his lips together tightly. Sol-leks was the first to struggle to his feet. Teek came after him. Joe was next, crying out in pain. Pike made agonizing attempts to rise. He collapsed twice while trying to get halfway up, and finally managed to stand on his third try. Buck didn't even try. He remained still where he had collapsed. The whip struck him repeatedly, but he didn't whimper or fight back. Thornton started forward several times as if he wanted to say something, but stopped himself. Tears formed in his eyes, and as the beating went on, he stood up and began pacing back and forth uncertainly.

This was the first time Buck had failed, which alone was enough to send Hal into a fury. He swapped the whip for his usual club. Buck refused to move despite the heavier blows that now rained down on him. Like his companions, he could barely stand up, but unlike them, he had decided he wouldn't get up. He had a dim sense that something terrible was about to happen. This feeling had been overwhelming when he'd pulled up to the riverbank, and it hadn't left him since. Given the thin and rotting ice he'd felt beneath his paws all day, it seemed he could sense catastrophe lurking just ahead on the ice where his master was trying to force him to go. He refused to budge. He had endured so much suffering and was so far gone that the blows barely hurt anymore. As they kept falling on him, the spark of life inside him flickered and dimmed. It was almost extinguished. He felt strangely detached. As if from a great distance, he was dimly aware that he was being beaten. The final traces of pain faded away. He no longer felt anything, though very faintly he could hear the sound of the club striking his body. But it no longer seemed like his body—it felt so far removed from him.

And then, suddenly, without any warning, John Thornton let out a wild, wordless cry that sounded more like an animal's roar and lunged at the man holding the club. Hal was thrown backward with such force that it seemed like a massive tree had crashed into him. Mercedes let out a piercing scream. Charles watched with a longing expression, wiping his tear-filled eyes, but remained seated because his body was too stiff to stand.

John Thornton stood over Buck, fighting to keep himself under control, too overwhelmed with fury to say a word.

"If you hit that dog again, I'll kill you," he finally managed to say in a strangled voice.

"It's my dog," Hal replied, wiping the blood from his mouth as he returned. "Get out of my way, or I'll deal with you. I'm heading to Dawson."

Thornton positioned himself between Hal and Buck, showing no signs of moving aside. Hal pulled out his long hunting knife. Mercedes let out screams, sobbed, burst into laughter, and displayed the wild chaos of hysteria. Thornton struck Hal's knuckles with the axe handle, sending the knife clattering to the ground. He hit his knuckles again when Hal attempted to retrieve it. Then Thornton bent down, picked up the knife himself, and with two quick cuts freed Buck from his harness.

Hal had given up completely. His hands were occupied with supporting his sister—or rather, his arms were—while Buck was too close to death to be any help pulling the sled. A few minutes later, they departed from the riverbank and headed down the river. Buck heard them leaving and lifted his head to watch. Pike was in the lead, Sol-leks was at the back, and Joe and Teek were positioned between them. They were all limping and stumbling. Mercedes was sitting on the loaded sled. Hal steered using the gee-pole, and Charles staggered along behind them.

As Buck observed them, Thornton knelt down next to him and used his rough but gentle hands to check for any broken bones. When his examination revealed nothing worse than numerous bruises and severe starvation, the sled had already traveled a quarter mile away. Both dog and man watched it moving slowly across the ice. All at once, they witnessed the rear of the sled sink down as if falling into a groove, and the steering pole, with Hal gripping it tightly, shot up into the air. Mercedes's terrified scream reached their ears. They watched Charles spin around and take a single step to rush back, but then an entire section of ice collapsed and both dogs and people vanished from sight. Only a gaping hole remained visible. The trail's foundation had completely given way.

John Thornton and Buck looked at each other.

"You poor devil," said John Thornton, and Buck licked his hand.

Chapter VI:
For the Love of a Man

When John Thornton had frozen his feet the previous December, his partners made him comfortable and left him to recover, while they continued up the river to cut and gather a raft of saw-logs for Dawson. He was still walking with a slight limp when he rescued Buck, but as the warm weather continued, even that minor limp disappeared. And here, resting by the riverbank throughout the long spring days, watching the flowing water and lazily listening to the birdsongs and the gentle sounds of nature, Buck gradually regained his strength.

A rest feels wonderful after traveling three thousand miles, and it's clear that Buck became lazy as his wounds healed, his muscles filled out, and flesh returned to cover his bones. In fact, they were all relaxing—Buck, John Thornton, and Skeet and Nig—waiting for the raft that would take them down to Dawson. Skeet was a small Irish setter who quickly became friends with Buck, who was too weak to resist her initial approaches when he was near death. She possessed the healing instinct that some dogs have; just as a mother cat cleans her kittens, she washed and tended to Buck's wounds. Every morning after he finished eating breakfast, she carried out this self-assigned duty, until he began anticipating her care as much as he looked forward to Thornton's attention. Nig, just as friendly but less expressive, was a massive black dog, part bloodhound and part deerhound, with cheerful eyes and unlimited good humor.

To Buck's amazement, these dogs showed no jealousy toward him. They appeared to share John Thornton's kindness and generous spirit. As Buck regained his strength, they drew him into all kinds of silly games, which Thornton himself couldn't resist joining. Through these playful activities, Buck enjoyed his recovery and entered a completely new way of life. For the first time, he experienced love—real, intense love. He had never felt anything like this during his time with Judge Miller in the sunny Santa Clara Valley. His relationship with the Judge's sons during hunting and hiking trips had been a working partnership. With the Judge's grandsons, it was more like dignified protection. And with Judge Miller himself, it had been a formal and respectful friendship. But the burning, passionate love—the kind that was worship, that bordered on obsession—only John Thornton had been able to awaken in him.

This man had saved his life, which was something significant; but beyond that, he was the perfect master. Other men took care of their dogs out of duty and practical business reasons; he cared for his dogs as if they were his own children, simply because he couldn't help himself. And he understood even more than that. He never forgot a kind greeting or an encouraging word, and sitting down for a lengthy conversation with them (he called it "gas") brought him as much pleasure as it did them. He had a habit of roughly taking Buck's head between his hands, resting his own head against Buck's, and shaking him back and forth, all the while calling him harsh names that Buck understood as terms of endearment. Buck experienced no greater happiness than that rough embrace and the sound of those muttered curses, and with each shake back and forth it felt as though his heart might burst from his chest, so intense was his joy. And when John Thornton finally let him go and Buck jumped to his feet, his mouth appearing to smile, his eyes full of expression, his throat trembling with sounds he couldn't make, and remained perfectly still in that position, John Thornton would say with deep respect, "God! you can almost speak!"

Buck had a way of showing love that seemed almost like he was trying to hurt someone. He would often grab Thornton's hand with his mouth and bite down so hard that the marks from his teeth would stay on the skin for quite a while afterward. Just as Buck understood that the curse words were actually expressions of love, Thornton understood that this pretend bite was really a sign of affection.

For the most part, however, Buck's love was expressed through adoration. While he became wild with happiness when Thornton touched him or spoke to him, he did not seek out these gestures. Unlike Skeet, who was inclined to push her nose under Thornton's hand and nudge repeatedly until she was petted, or Nig, who would approach and rest his massive head on Thornton's knee, Buck was satisfied to worship from a distance. He would lie for hours, eager and alert, at Thornton's feet, gazing up into his face, focusing on it, examining it, following with intense interest each passing expression, every movement or shift of feature. Or, depending on the circumstances, he would lie further away, to the side or behind, observing the outline of the man and the occasional movements of his body. And frequently, such was the connection in which they existed, the intensity of Buck's stare would cause John Thornton's head to turn around, and he would meet the gaze, without words, his heart radiating from his eyes as Buck's heart radiated from his own.

For a long time following his rescue, Buck refused to let Thornton leave his sight. From the instant Thornton stepped out of the tent until he returned, Buck stayed close behind him. The temporary owners he'd had since arriving in the Northland had created in him a deep worry that no owner would stay with him forever. He feared that Thornton would disappear from his life just as Perrault and François and the Scottish half-breed had vanished. Even during the night, while dreaming, this fear troubled him. During these moments, he would wake himself up and crawl through the cold air to the tent opening, where he would stand quietly and listen to his master breathing.

Despite his deep love for John Thornton, which seemed to reflect a gentling, civilizing influence, the primitive instincts that the northern wilderness had awakened in him stayed strong and vibrant. He possessed loyalty and devotion, qualities forged by hearth and home, but he kept his untamed nature and cunning. He was a creature of the wilderness who had come in from the wild to rest beside John Thornton's fire, not a domesticated dog from the comfortable South shaped by countless generations of civilization. His profound love prevented him from stealing from this man, but he wouldn't hesitate for a moment to take from any other person in any other camp, and his cleverness in stealing allowed him to avoid getting caught.

His face and body bore the scars from countless dog bites, yet he fought with greater ferocity and cunning than ever before. Skeet and Nig were too gentle by nature to pick fights—and besides, they belonged to John Thornton; but any unfamiliar dog, regardless of its breed or courage, quickly recognized Buck's dominance or found itself fighting for survival against a ruthless opponent. Buck showed no mercy. He had thoroughly mastered the brutal law of violence and force, never giving up an advantage or backing down from an enemy he had marked for death. He had learned from Spitz and from the toughest fighting dogs in the police and postal services, understanding there could be no compromise. He had to dominate or be dominated; showing compassion was a sign of weakness. Compassion had no place in this ancient way of life. It was mistaken for fear, and such confusion led to death. The rule was kill or be killed, devour or be devoured; and this ancient command, emerging from the deepest reaches of time, he followed without question.

He was older than the days he had lived and the breaths he had taken. He connected the past with the present, and the eternity stretching behind him pulsed through him in a powerful rhythm that moved him like the tides and seasons moved. He sat beside John Thornton's fire, a broad-chested dog with white fangs and long fur; but behind him were the spirits of all kinds of dogs, half-wolves and wild wolves, pressing and urging, tasting the flavor of the meat he ate, thirsting for the water he drank, smelling the wind with him, listening with him and telling him the sounds made by the wild creatures in the forest, controlling his moods, guiding his actions, lying down to sleep with him when he rested, and dreaming with him and beyond him and becoming the very substance of his dreams.

These shadowy figures called to him so insistently that each day humanity and human concerns grew more distant from him. Deep within the forest, a call echoed, and whenever he heard this mysterious, thrilling, and enticing sound, he felt driven to turn away from the fire and the well-worn ground surrounding it, and to dive into the forest, deeper and deeper, not knowing where or why he was going; he didn't question where or why, as the call rang out commandingly from deep within the forest. Yet whenever he reached the soft, untouched earth and the green shadows, his love for John Thornton pulled him back to the fire once more.

Thornton was the only person who truly mattered to him. Everyone else meant absolutely nothing. Random travelers might compliment or show him affection, but he remained emotionally distant through it all, and if someone became too pushy with their attention, he would simply stand up and walk away. When Thornton's business partners, Hans and Pete, finally arrived on the long-awaited raft, Buck completely ignored them until he realized they were close friends of Thornton's; only then did he begin to tolerate their presence in a detached manner, accepting their kindness as if he were doing them a favor by allowing it. These men were cut from the same cloth as Thornton—rugged outdoorsmen who lived simply, thought straightforwardly, and saw things clearly; and before they guided the raft into the large swirling pool near the sawmill at Dawson, they had figured out Buck's personality and behavior patterns, understanding not to expect the kind of close friendship he shared with Skeet and Nig.

Buck's love for Thornton continued to deepen and intensify. Among all the men Buck had known, Thornton was the only one who could strap a pack onto Buck's back during summer travels. There was nothing too difficult for Buck to accomplish when Thornton gave the order. One day, after they had funded themselves with money from selling the raft and departed Dawson heading toward the headwaters of the Tanana River, the men and dogs were resting on top of a cliff that dropped straight down to bare bedrock three hundred feet below. John Thornton sat close to the edge with Buck positioned at his shoulder. A careless impulse suddenly took hold of Thornton, and he called Hans and Pete's attention to the test he was considering. "Jump, Buck!" he ordered, sweeping his arm outward over the deep gorge. In the following moment, he found himself wrestling with Buck right at the cliff's edge, while Hans and Pete pulled them both back to safety.

"It's eerie," Pete said, after it was finished and they had caught their breath.

Thornton shook his head. "No, it's magnificent, and it's terrifying at the same time. You know, sometimes it actually scares me."

"I don't want to be the guy who puts his hands on you while he's here," Pete declared firmly, gesturing toward Buck with his head.

"By Jingo!" was Hans's contribution. "Not myself either."

It was at Circle City, before the year ended, that Pete's fears came true. "Black" Burton, a man with a nasty temper and a mean streak, had been trying to start a fight with a newcomer at the bar, when Thornton stepped in good-naturedly to break it up. Buck, following his usual habit, was lying in a corner with his head resting on his paws, watching every move his master made. Burton threw a punch without any warning, delivering it straight from his shoulder. Thornton went spinning and only kept himself from falling by grabbing onto the bar rail.

Those watching heard a sound that wasn't quite a bark or a yelp, but something best described as a roar, and they witnessed Buck's body launch into the air as he sprang from the floor toward Burton's throat. The man saved his life by instinctively throwing up his arm, but he was thrown backward to the ground with Buck on top of him. Buck released his teeth from the man's arm and lunged again for the throat. This time the man only managed to partially block the attack, and his throat was ripped open. Then the crowd swarmed Buck, driving him away; but while a doctor stopped the bleeding, Buck paced back and forth, snarling with rage, trying to charge forward, only to be pushed back by a wall of threatening clubs. A "miners' meeting," organized right there on the spot, determined that the dog had been sufficiently provoked, and Buck was cleared of wrongdoing. However, his reputation was established, and from that moment forward his name became known throughout every camp in Alaska.

Later that fall, he saved John Thornton's life in a completely different way. The three partners were guiding a long, narrow poling-boat down a dangerous stretch of rapids on Forty-Mile Creek. Hans and Pete walked along the riverbank, securing the boat with a thin Manila rope tied from tree to tree, while Thornton stayed in the boat, controlling its descent with a pole and calling out instructions to those on shore. Buck remained on the bank, worried and anxious, staying alongside the boat and never taking his eyes off his master.

At a particularly dangerous spot, where a ridge of barely underwater rocks extended into the river, Hans released the rope, and while Thornton used a pole to push the boat out into the current, he ran along the bank holding the rope's end to stop the boat once it had passed the rocky ledge. The boat did clear the obstacle and was racing downstream in a current as fast as rushing mill water, when Hans suddenly jerked it to a halt with the rope. The boat flipped over and crashed into the bank upside down, while Thornton, thrown completely out of it, was swept downstream toward the most treacherous section of the rapids, a stretch of violent water where no swimmer could survive.

Buck had leaped into action immediately, and after covering three hundred yards through the churning water, he caught up with Thornton. When Buck felt Thornton grab hold of his tail, he turned toward the shore, swimming with every ounce of his magnificent strength. However, their movement toward the bank was painfully slow, while their drift downstream was alarmingly fast. From below came the deadly thundering sound where the wild current became even more violent and was torn apart into fragments and mist by the rocks that jutted up like the teeth of a massive comb. The pull of the water as it began the final steep descent was terrifying, and Thornton realized that reaching the shore was hopeless. He scraped violently across one rock, was battered against a second, and slammed into a third with bone-crushing impact. He gripped its wet, slippery surface with both hands, letting go of Buck, and over the thunderous noise of the turbulent water yelled: "Go, Buck! Go!"

Buck couldn't maintain his position and was carried downstream, fighting frantically but unable to regain his footing. When he heard Thornton's command called out again, he partially lifted himself from the water, raising his head high as if taking one final look, then obediently turned toward the shore. He swam with great strength and was pulled to safety by Pete and Hans at the exact spot where swimming became impossible and certain death awaited.

They understood that a person could only hold onto a slippery rock against such a powerful current for just a few minutes, so they sprinted up the riverbank as quickly as possible to a spot well upstream from where Thornton was desperately clinging. They secured the rope they had been using to control the boat around Buck's neck and shoulders, taking care to position it so it wouldn't choke him or interfere with his ability to swim, then sent him into the rushing water. He began swimming with determination, but his angle into the current wasn't quite right. He realized his error too late, just as Thornton came alongside him only a few strokes away, while the current swept him helplessly downstream.

Hans quickly secured the rope, treating Buck like a boat being moored. As the rope tightened around him in the rushing current, Buck was pulled beneath the water's surface, where he stayed until his body hit the riverbank and he was dragged out. He was nearly drowned, and Hans and

Pete immediately threw themselves on top of him, pounding his chest to force air back into his lungs and push the water out. Buck struggled to stand but collapsed again. The weak sound of Thornton's voice reached them, and although they couldn't understand his words, they realized he was in desperate trouble. Hearing his master's voice hit Buck like a bolt of electricity. He jumped to his feet and raced up the bank, getting ahead of the men as he returned to the spot where he had originally entered the water.

Once more the rope was fastened and he was sent out, and once more he began swimming, but this time he headed directly into the current. He had made an error in judgment before, but he wouldn't make the same mistake twice. Hans let out the rope, keeping it taut without any slack, while Pete made sure it stayed free of tangles. Buck held his position until he was positioned directly upstream from Thornton; then he turned around, and with the velocity of a speeding locomotive rushed down toward him. Thornton spotted him approaching, and as Buck collided with him like a massive battering ram, with the entire force of the rushing water propelling him forward, he reached upward and wrapped both arms tightly around the thick, furry neck. Hans quickly wound the rope around the tree trunk, and both Buck and Thornton were suddenly pulled beneath the surface. Choking and gasping for air, sometimes one on top and sometimes the other, being dragged across the sharp, uneven riverbed, crashing into boulders and fallen branches, they swung toward the shoreline.

Thornton regained consciousness lying face down, with Hans and Pete forcefully pushing him back and forth across a fallen tree trunk. The first thing he looked for was Buck, whose motionless and seemingly dead body had Nig howling over it, while Skeet was licking his wet face and shut eyes. Thornton himself was bruised and beaten up, and once he had recovered, he carefully examined Buck's body, discovering three fractured ribs.

"That settles it," he announced. "We're making camp right here." And that's exactly what they did, staying put until Buck's ribs healed and he could travel again.

That winter in Dawson, Buck accomplished another remarkable feat that, while perhaps not as heroic as his previous exploits, elevated his reputation significantly in the ranks of Alaskan legend. This achievement was especially satisfying to the three men because they desperately needed the equipment it would provide, and it would allow them to take the long-awaited journey into the untouched eastern territory, where prospectors had not yet ventured. The whole thing started with a conversation at the Eldorado Saloon, where men were bragging about their prized dogs. Because of his impressive track record, Buck became the focus of these men's challenges, forcing Thornton to vigorously defend his dog's abilities. After thirty minutes of heated discussion, one man claimed his dog could get a sled moving with five hundred pounds loaded on it and pull it away; another boasted that his dog could handle six hundred pounds; and a third insisted his could manage seven hundred.

"Come on!" said John Thornton; "Buck can pull a thousand pounds."

"And break it loose? And walk away with it for a hundred yards?" demanded Matthewson, a Bonanza King, the one who had boasted of seven hundred.

"And break it loose, and pull it for a hundred yards," John Thornton said calmly.

"Well," Matthewson said, speaking slowly and clearly so everyone could hear him, "I've got a thousand dollars that says he can't do it. And here's the money." As he said this, he slammed a sack of gold dust about the size of a bologna sausage down on the bar.

Nobody said a word. Thornton's bold challenge, if that's what it was, had been accepted. He could feel the heat of embarrassment rising in his cheeks. His mouth had gotten him into trouble. He wasn't sure if Buck could actually pull a thousand pounds. Half a ton! The sheer size of it overwhelmed him. He had complete confidence in Buck's power and had frequently believed the dog was strong enough to move such a weight; but never before, like right now, had he confronted the actual possibility of it happening, with a dozen pairs of eyes staring at him, quiet and expectant. What's more, he didn't have a thousand dollars; neither did Hans or Pete.

"I have a sled sitting outside right now with twenty fifty-pound sacks of flour loaded on it," Matthewson continued with harsh bluntness, "so don't let that stop you."

Thornton remained silent. He couldn't find the words. He looked from one face to another with the distant expression of someone whose mind had gone blank and was desperately searching for something to jumpstart his thoughts again. His gaze landed on Jim O'Brien's face, a Mastodon King and longtime friend. It served as a prompt for him, appearing to awaken him to take action he never would have imagined taking.

"Can you lend me a thousand?" he asked, almost in a whisper.

"Absolutely," O'Brien replied, dropping a bulging sack next to Matthewson's with a heavy thud. "Though I have to say, John, I don't have much confidence that the animal can pull this off."

The Eldorado emptied its customers onto the street to witness the test. The tables sat abandoned, and the dealers and gamekeepers emerged to observe the outcome of the bet and place their own wagers. Several hundred men, dressed in furs and mittens, gathered around the sled within close range. Matthewson's sled, carrying a thousand pounds of flour, had been sitting there for several hours, and in the brutal cold (it was sixty degrees below zero) the runners had frozen solid to the hard-packed snow. Men offered two-to-one odds that Buck couldn't move the sled. An argument broke out over the meaning of "break out." O'Brien argued it was Thornton's right to knock the runners free, leaving Buck to "break it out" from a complete stop. Matthewson maintained that the phrase meant breaking the runners loose from the frozen grip of the snow. Most of the men who had witnessed the making of the wager sided with him, which raised the odds to three to one against Buck.

Nobody stepped forward to take the bet. Not a single person believed he could pull off such an incredible feat. Thornton had been rushed into making the wager and was filled with uncertainty; now, as he stared at the actual sled sitting there in front of him, with the usual team of ten dogs lying curled up in the snow nearby, the challenge seemed even more impossible than before. Matthewson grew increasingly excited and confident.

"Three to one!" he announced. "I'll bet you another thousand at those odds, Thornton. What do you say?"

Doubt was clearly written across Thornton's face, but his fighting spirit had awakened—that fierce determination that rises above unfavorable odds, refuses to acknowledge what cannot be done, and hears nothing except the call to battle. He summoned Hans and Pete to his side. Their wallets were nearly empty, and combining his money with theirs, the three partners could only scrape together two hundred dollars. At this low point in their luck, this amount represented everything they owned; nevertheless, they put it forward without hesitation to match against Matthewson's six hundred dollars.

The team of ten dogs was unhitched, and Buck, wearing his own harness, was placed into the sled. He had been swept up by the infectious excitement, and he sensed that somehow he needed to accomplish something extraordinary for John Thornton. Whispers of awe at his magnificent appearance rippled through the crowd. He was in flawless condition, without a single ounce of excess weight, and the one hundred and fifty pounds he carried were pure determination and strength. His thick coat gleamed with a silky luster. Along his neck and across his shoulders, his mane, even while at rest, seemed partially raised and appeared to move with his every motion, as if his abundant energy brought each individual hair to life. His broad chest and powerful front legs were perfectly proportioned to the rest of his frame, where his muscles formed tight bands beneath his skin. People touched these muscles and declared them as hard as steel, and the betting odds dropped to two to one.

"Good God, sir! Good God, sir!" stammered a member of the newest ruling family, a king of the Skookum Benches. "I'm offering you eight hundred for him, sir, before the test, sir; eight hundred just as he is right now."

Thornton shook his head and moved to Buck's side.

"You need to step back from him," Matthewson objected. "Give him space to move freely and plenty of room."

The crowd went quiet; the only sounds were the voices of gamblers desperately offering two-to-one odds.

Everyone recognized that Buck was a magnificent animal, but twenty fifty-pound sacks of flour seemed like too much money for them to risk opening their wallets.

Thornton dropped to his knees beside Buck. He cradled Buck's head between his hands and pressed his cheek against the dog's. He didn't shake him playfully like he usually did, or whisper those gentle, affectionate words he was known for; instead, he spoke quietly into Buck's ear. "Because you love me, Buck. Because you love me," he whispered. Buck whimpered with barely contained excitement.

The crowd watched with curiosity. The situation was becoming mysterious. It felt like magic. When Thornton stood up, Buck grabbed his mittened hand between his jaws, pressing down with his teeth and letting go slowly, almost reluctantly. This was his response, expressed not through words, but through love. Thornton took several steps back.

"Now, Buck," he said.

Buck pulled the harness tight, then loosened it by a few inches. This was the method he had been taught.

"Wow!" Thornton's voice cut through the air, piercing the heavy silence.

Buck veered sharply to the right, completing the motion with a sudden dive that pulled the rope tight and abruptly stopped his one hundred and fifty pounds of weight. The sled trembled, and a sharp crackling sound emerged from beneath the runners.

"Haw!" Thornton commanded.

Buck repeated the same move, this time turning to the left. The crackling sound became a sharp snapping, and the sled swiveled while its runners slid and scraped several inches sideways. The sled broke free. The men held their breath, completely unaware they were doing so.

"Now, MUSH!"

Thornton's command exploded like a gunshot. Buck launched himself forward, pulling the harness tight with a bone-jarring thrust. His entire body coiled together in the massive effort, muscles twisting and bunching like living creatures beneath his glossy coat. His broad chest dropped low to the ground, his head thrust forward and down, while his paws flew frantically, claws cutting parallel lines in the hard-packed snow. The sled rocked and shook, beginning to move forward. One of his paws lost its grip, and someone let out a pained groan. Then the sled jerked ahead in what seemed like a quick series of starts and stops, though it never truly halted again...half an inch...an inch...two inches... The jerking movements gradually lessened; as the sled picked up speed, he matched its rhythm, until it was gliding smoothly forward.

Men gasped and started breathing again, not realizing they had momentarily stopped breathing. Thornton was running behind, cheering Buck on with brief, encouraging words. The distance had been marked out, and as he approached the pile of firewood that indicated the end of the hundred yards, a cheer started to build and build, which exploded into a roar as he passed the firewood and stopped on command. Every man was breaking free, even Matthewson. Hats and mittens were flying through the air. Men were shaking hands, it didn't matter with whom, and overflowing with excitement in a general jumbled chatter.

But Thornton dropped to his knees next to Buck. He pressed his head against Buck's head, gently rocking him back and forth. The people who rushed over could hear him swearing at Buck, and he continued cursing him with deep emotion, his voice both tender and full of love.

"Good God, sir! Good God, sir!" stammered the Skookum Bench king. "I'll give you a thousand for him, sir, a thousand, sir—twelve hundred, sir."

Thornton stood up. His eyes were filled with tears. The tears flowed openly down his face. "Sir," he said to the Skookum Bench king, "no, sir. You can go to hell, sir. That's the best I can offer you, sir."

Buck gripped Thornton's hand gently between his teeth. Thornton playfully shook him back and forth. As if moved by the same instinct, the spectators stepped back to give them space, and they were careful not to intrude on the moment again.

Chapter VII:
The Sounding of the Call

When Buck earned sixteen hundred dollars in five minutes for John Thornton, he enabled his master to settle outstanding debts and travel with his partners into the East in search of a legendary lost mine whose story was as ancient as the region itself. Countless men had searched for it; only a handful had discovered it; and many others never came back from their pursuit. This lost mine was filled with tragedy and wrapped in mystery. Nobody knew who the first man was. The oldest stories ended before reaching back to him. From the very beginning, there had been an old and deteriorating cabin. Dying men had testified to its existence, and to the mine whose location it indicated, supporting their claims with gold nuggets that were different from any known type of gold found in the Northland.

But no living person had plundered this treasure vault, and the dead remained dead; therefore John Thornton and Pete and Hans, along with Buck and half a dozen other dogs, headed eastward on an unfamiliar trail to succeed where men and dogs as capable as themselves had failed. They traveled seventy miles by sled up the Yukon, turned left into the Stewart River, passed the Mayo and the McQuestion, and continued until the Stewart itself became a small stream, winding through the towering peaks that formed the spine of the continent.

John Thornton demanded very little from people or the natural world. The wilderness held no fear for him. Armed with just a pinch of salt and his rifle, he could venture deep into the untamed lands and go wherever he wanted for as long as he chose. Never rushing, he followed the ways of the Native Americans, hunting for his meals during his daily travels; and when he came up empty-handed, like the indigenous people, he simply continued his journey, confident that eventually he would find food. Therefore, on this grand expedition toward the East, fresh meat served as the main course, ammunition and equipment formed the bulk of what the sled carried, and his schedule stretched into the endless days ahead.

For Buck, this life of hunting, fishing, and endless wandering through unfamiliar territories brought immense joy. They would travel steadily for weeks at a time, day after day, then set up camp for weeks on end in various locations while the dogs rested and the men melted holes through frozen mud and gravel, washing countless pans of dirt beside the warmth of their fires. At times they went without food, while other times they ate abundantly, depending entirely on how plentiful the game was and how successful their hunting proved to be. When summer came, both dogs and men carried supplies on their backs, crossed crystal-blue mountain lakes on rafts, and navigated unknown rivers in narrow boats they had cut from the surrounding forest.

The months passed by, and they wandered back and forth through the unmapped wilderness, where no people lived yet where people had once been if the Lost Cabin story was real. They crossed mountain passes during summer snowstorms, trembled beneath the midnight sun on bare peaks between the tree line and the permanent snow, descended into summer valleys filled with swarms of gnats and flies, and in the shade of glaciers gathered strawberries and flowers as fresh and beautiful as any the South could offer. When autumn arrived, they entered a strange lake region, somber and quiet, where waterfowl had once lived, but where now there was no life or trace of life—only the howling of cold winds, the formation of ice in protected spots, and the sad lapping of waves against deserted shores.

And through another winter they wandered along the faded trails of men who had traveled before them. Once, they discovered a path cut through the forest, an old path, and the Lost Cabin felt very close. But the path started nowhere and led nowhere, and it stayed a mystery, just as the man who created it and his reasons for making it stayed a mystery. Another time they stumbled upon the weathered remains of a hunting lodge, and among the pieces of decayed blankets John Thornton discovered a long-barreled flintlock. He recognized it as a Hudson Bay Company gun from the early days in the Northwest, when such a gun was worth its height in beaver pelts stacked flat. And that was everything—no clue about the man who in an earlier time had built the lodge and left the gun among the blankets.

Spring arrived once again, and after all their wandering, they discovered not the Lost Cabin, but a shallow gold deposit in a wide valley where the precious metal gleamed like golden butter across the bottom of their washing pan. They searched no further. Every day of work brought them thousands of dollars in pure gold dust and nuggets, and they labored daily without rest. The gold was stored in moose-hide sacks, fifty pounds per bag, and stacked like cordwood outside their spruce-branch shelter. They worked like titans, with days rushing past like fleeting dreams as they accumulated their fortune.

The dogs had nothing to do except occasionally drag in the meat that Thornton had killed, and Buck spent countless hours lost in thought beside the fire. The image of the short-legged, hairy man appeared to him more often now that there was hardly any work to occupy his time; and frequently, as he sat blinking in the firelight, Buck would journey with this figure into that other world he still remembered.

The most striking feature of this other world appeared to be fear. When Buck observed the hairy man sleeping beside the fire, his head resting between his knees and hands clasped overhead, Buck noticed that his sleep was troubled, filled with frequent jolts and sudden awakenings, during which he would look anxiously into the darkness and throw more wood onto the fire. Whether they walked along the shoreline of a sea, where the hairy man collected shellfish and consumed them as he gathered them, he did so with eyes that constantly scanned everywhere for concealed danger and with legs ready to flee like the wind at the first sign of threat. Through the forest they moved silently, Buck following close behind the hairy man; and both of them remained alert and watchful, their ears twitching and shifting and their nostrils trembling, because the man could hear and smell just as sharply as Buck. The hairy man was able to leap up into the trees and move forward just as quickly as he could on the ground, swinging by his arms from branch to branch, sometimes spanning distances of a dozen feet, releasing and grasping, never falling, never losing his hold. Indeed, he appeared just as comfortable among the trees as he was on the ground; and Buck retained memories of nights spent keeping watch beneath trees where the hairy man perched, gripping tightly as he slept.

And closely connected to the visions of the hairy man was the call that continued echoing in the depths of the forest. It filled him with tremendous restlessness and unusual longings. It made him feel an unclear, sweet happiness, and he experienced wild cravings and impulses for something he couldn't identify. Sometimes he chased the call into the forest, searching for it as if it were something he could touch, barking quietly or boldly, depending on his mood. He would push his nose into the cool forest moss, or into the dark earth where tall grasses grew, and breathe in deeply with delight at the rich earth scents; or he would crouch for hours, as if hiding, behind moss-covered trunks of fallen trees, alert and listening to everything that moved and made sounds around him. It could be that, lying in this way, he hoped to catch this call he couldn't comprehend. But he didn't understand why he did these different things. He felt driven to do them, and didn't think about them at all.

Irresistible urges would suddenly take hold of him. He might be resting in camp, drowsing peacefully in the afternoon heat, when all at once his head would snap up and his ears would prick forward, alert and focused, and he would leap to his feet and race away, running for hours through the forest corridors and across the clearings where the grass grew in thick clumps. He delighted in racing down dried creek beds, and in stalking and observing the birds that lived in the woods. He would spend entire days hidden in the thick brush where he could watch the grouse beating their wings and parading back and forth. Most of all, though, he loved to run during the soft twilight of summer nights, listening to the quiet, drowsy sounds of the forest, interpreting the signs and noises the way a person might read a book, and searching for that mysterious presence that beckoned—beckoned to him constantly, whether he was awake or asleep, calling him to come.

One night he jolted awake suddenly, his eyes bright and alert, nostrils fluttering as they caught a scent, his mane rising in rolling waves. From the forest came the call—or one note of it, since the call had many notes—clearer and more definite than ever before: a long, drawn-out howl that resembled, yet differed from, any sound made by a husky dog. And he recognized it in that ancient, familiar way, as a sound he had heard before. He leaped through the sleeping camp and raced silently through the woods. As he got closer to the cry, he moved more cautiously, being careful with every step, until he reached a clearing among the trees, and looking out he saw, sitting upright on its haunches with its nose pointed toward the sky, a long, lean timber wolf.

He hadn't made a sound, but the creature stopped howling and tried to detect where he was. Buck stepped into the clearing, crouching low with his body tensed and ready, his tail held straight and rigid, placing each paw with unusual caution. Every gesture conveyed both a threat and an invitation to be friends. This was the dangerous peace that occurs when wild predators encounter each other. However, the wolf ran away as soon as it saw him. Buck chased after it with wild bounds, desperate to catch up. He cornered the wolf in a dead-end ravine along the creek bed where fallen logs blocked any escape route. The wolf spun around, balancing on its back legs just like Joe and all trapped sled dogs do, growling and bristling while snapping its jaws together in a rapid, continuous series of bites.

Buck didn't attack, but instead moved in circles around him and surrounded him with friendly gestures. The wolf remained suspicious and frightened; Buck weighed three times as much as he did, and the wolf's head barely came up to Buck's shoulder. Looking for his opportunity, he bolted away, and the pursuit began again. Repeatedly he found himself trapped, and the same pattern played out, though he was in weak condition, or Buck wouldn't have been able to catch up with him so easily. He would keep running until Buck's head drew level with his side, then he would spin around to face him defensively, only to bolt away again as soon as he saw the chance.

But eventually Buck's persistence paid off; the wolf, realizing that no harm was meant, finally touched noses with him. Then they became friends, and romped around in the cautious, somewhat shy manner that fierce creatures use to mask their wildness. After playing like this for a while, the wolf trotted off at a relaxed pace in a way that clearly indicated he had a destination in mind. He signaled to Buck that he should follow, and they ran together through the dim twilight, directly up the creek bed, into the canyon where it originated, and over the barren ridge where it began.

On the opposite slope of the watershed, they descended into flat terrain filled with vast stretches of forest and numerous streams, and through these expansive woodlands they ran without stopping, hour after hour, as the sun climbed higher and the day became warmer. Buck felt wildly joyful. He understood that he was finally responding to the call, running alongside his forest companion toward the place where the call undoubtedly originated. Ancient memories flooded back to him rapidly, and he was responding to them just as he once responded to the actual experiences they represented. He had experienced this before, somewhere in that other, vaguely remembered existence, and he was experiencing it again now, running freely in the wilderness, the soft earth beneath his feet, the vast sky above him.

They paused beside a flowing stream to drink water, and while resting there, Buck's thoughts turned to John Thornton. He settled down on the ground. The wolf continued moving toward the source of the mysterious call, but then came back to Buck, touching noses with him and behaving as if trying to urge him forward. However, Buck turned around and began walking slowly back the way he had come. For most of an hour, his wild companion ran alongside him, making soft whimpering sounds. Eventually, the wolf sat down, lifted his muzzle toward the sky, and let out a long howl. The sound was filled with sadness, and as Buck continued steadily on his path, he listened to the howling become weaker and more distant until it finally disappeared completely.

John Thornton was having dinner when Buck burst into the camp and leaped on him with wild affection, knocking him over, climbing all over him, licking his face, and gently biting his hand—"acting like a complete fool," as John Thornton described it, while he playfully shook Buck back and forth and cursed at him with love.

For two days and nights, Buck stayed close to camp and wouldn't let Thornton leave his sight. He trailed behind him during work, observed him eating his meals, watched him crawl into his bedroll at night and emerge from it each morning. However, after those two days passed, the wilderness call started echoing through the forest with greater urgency than before. Buck's anxiety returned, and memories of his wild companion haunted him, along with visions of the beautiful territory beyond the mountain pass and their shared runs through the vast woodland expanses. He began roaming the forest once more, but his wild companion never appeared again; and despite keeping long, watchful vigils and listening intently, he never heard that sorrowful howl again.

He started sleeping outdoors at night, staying away from camp for days on end; and once he crossed the ridge at the source of the creek and descended into the region of forests and waterways. There he roamed for a week, searching unsuccessfully for fresh traces of his wild companion, hunting his food as he traveled and moving with the long, effortless stride that never seems to grow weary. He caught salmon in a wide river that flowed somewhere toward the ocean, and beside this river he killed a massive black bear, blinded by mosquitoes while also fishing, and thrashing through the woods helpless and fearsome. Even so, it was a fierce battle, and it awakened the final dormant traces of Buck's savagery. And two days afterward, when he came back to his kill and discovered a dozen wolverines fighting over the remains, he drove them away like dust; and those that escaped left two behind who would fight no more.

The craving for blood grew more intense than it had ever been. He had become a predator, a creature that hunted for survival, feeding on other living beings, relying entirely on his own power and skill to thrive successfully in a harsh world where only the strongest could endure. All of this filled him with an immense sense of self-pride that spread through his entire physical form like an infection. This confidence showed itself in every movement he made, was visible in the flex of each muscle, communicated as clearly as spoken words through his posture, and made his magnificent fur coat even more spectacular. Except for the scattered brown markings on his snout and above his eyes, and the streak of white fur running down the center of his chest, he could easily have been taken for an enormous wolf, bigger than any wolf that had ever existed. From his St. Bernard father he had gained his massive size and bulk, but it was his shepherd mother who had shaped that size and bulk into its current form. His snout had the elongated shape of a wolf's muzzle, except that it was much larger than any wolf's muzzle could be; and his head, which was somewhat wider, resembled a wolf's head but on a much grander scale.

His cunning was the cunning of a wolf, wild and untamed; his intelligence was that of a shepherd and a St. Bernard combined; and all of this, along with experience gained in the harshest of environments, made him as dangerous a creature as any that wandered the wilderness. A meat-eating animal surviving on pure flesh, he was in his prime, at the peak of his existence, overflowing with strength and vitality. When Thornton ran a gentle hand along his back, sparks and crackling sounds followed his touch, each hair releasing its stored energy at the contact. Every part of him—brain and body, nerve tissue and muscle fiber—was tuned to the highest level of sensitivity; and between all these parts there existed perfect balance and harmony. To sights and sounds and situations that demanded action, he reacted with lightning speed. As quickly as a husky could leap to defend against an attack or to strike, he could leap twice as fast. He spotted the movement or caught the sound and reacted in less time than another dog needed just to see or hear. He noticed, decided, and acted in the same moment. In reality, the three actions of noticing, deciding, and acting happened one after another; but the time gaps between them were so tiny that they seemed to occur all at once. His muscles were filled with energy and sprang into action sharply, like steel coils. Life flowed through him in magnificent waves, joyful and wild, until it felt like it might tear him apart in pure bliss and spill out generously across the world.

"There has never been a dog like that," John Thornton said one day, as he and his partners watched Buck walking out of camp.

"When he was made, the mold was broken," said Pete.

"By jingo! I think so myself," Hans affirmed.

They saw him walking out of camp, but they didn't witness the immediate and dramatic change that happened once he entered the privacy of the forest. He stopped walking normally. Instantly he transformed into a creature of the wilderness, moving silently with cat-like steps, becoming a fleeting shadow that appeared and vanished among the other shadows. He understood how to use every bit of cover available, how to crawl on his stomach like a snake, and like a snake how to spring forward and attack. He could snatch a ptarmigan right from its nest, kill a sleeping rabbit, and catch the small chipmunks in midair when they fled just a moment too late toward the trees. Fish swimming in open pools weren't fast enough to escape him, and even cautious beavers repairing their dams couldn't avoid him. He killed for food, not out of cruelty, but he preferred to eat what he had hunted himself. A playful streak ran through his actions, and he took pleasure in sneaking up on squirrels and, just when he almost had them, letting them escape while they chattered in terror as they fled to the treetops.

As autumn arrived, moose began appearing in much larger numbers, making their way slowly down to spend the winter in the lower, milder valleys. Buck had already brought down a wandering young calf that wasn't fully grown, but he had a strong desire for bigger and more challenging prey, and he found exactly what he was looking for one day on the ridge at the source of the creek. A group of twenty moose had come across from the region of waterways and forests, and leading them was an enormous bull. The animal was in a fierce mood, and standing more than six feet tall, he was as intimidating an opponent as Buck could have hoped for. The bull swung his massive flat antlers back and forth, which spread out into fourteen points and measured seven feet from tip to tip. His small eyes glowed with a cruel and angry light, while he bellowed with rage at the sight of Buck.

From the bull's side, just ahead of the flank, stuck out the feathered end of an arrow, which explained his fierce behavior. Following an instinct that came from ancient hunting days of the prehistoric world, Buck began to separate the bull from the herd. This was no easy job. He would bark and dart around in front of the bull, staying just beyond reach of the massive antlers and the dangerous splayed hooves that could crush his life with one strike. Unable to turn away from this fanged threat and continue on, the bull became consumed with fury. During these moments he rushed at Buck, who pulled back cleverly, drawing him forward by pretending he couldn't get away. But when the bull was cut off from his companions this way, two or three of the younger bulls would rush back at Buck and allow the injured bull to return to the herd.

There exists a wild patience—stubborn, relentless, enduring as life itself—that keeps the spider motionless in its web for countless hours, holds the snake still in its coils, and freezes the panther in its hiding place; this patience is uniquely characteristic of life when it hunts for its survival; and this same patience belonged to Buck as he stayed close to the edge of the herd, slowing down their movement, provoking the young bulls, harassing the cows with their partially grown calves, and driving the injured bull into a frenzy of powerless fury. This went on for half a day. Buck seemed to be everywhere at once, striking from every direction, surrounding the herd in a storm of threat, separating his target as quickly as it could return to its companions, exhausting the patience of the hunted animals, which is a weaker patience than that of the hunters.

As the day progressed and the sun sank toward its resting place in the northwest (darkness had returned and the autumn nights stretched for six hours), the young bulls grew increasingly hesitant to return and help their embattled leader. The approaching winter was driving them toward the lower elevations, and it appeared they could never escape this relentless creature that kept holding them back. Furthermore, it wasn't the survival of the herd or the young bulls that was at stake. Only the life of a single member was being demanded, which concerned them far less than their own survival, and ultimately they were willing to pay that price.

As evening approached, the aging bull stood with his head hanging low, watching his companions—the cows he had known for years, the calves he had sired, and the bulls he had dominated—as they moved quickly away through the dimming light. He couldn't follow them because in front of him crouched the ruthless, sharp-toothed predator that wouldn't allow him to escape. Weighing over fifteen hundred pounds, more than three-quarters of a ton, he had lived a long and powerful life filled with battles and challenges, and now at the end he confronted death from the jaws of a creature whose head barely reached his massive, bony knees.

From that point forward, day and night, Buck stayed with his prey constantly, refusing to give it even a moment of peace, preventing it from eating the leaves from trees or the tender shoots of young birch and willow. He also denied the injured bull any chance to satisfy its intense thirst at the narrow flowing streams they encountered. Frequently, driven by desperation, the moose would break into extended periods of running. During these times Buck made no effort to stop him, instead running effortlessly behind him, content with how the hunt was progressing, resting when the moose stopped moving, and attacking him aggressively whenever he tried to eat or drink.

The massive head drooped lower and lower beneath its crown of antlers, and the unsteady trot became increasingly feeble. The moose began standing motionless for extended periods, nose pressed to the earth with dejected ears hanging limp, giving Buck more opportunities to drink water and rest. During these moments, as he panted with his red tongue hanging out and kept his eyes locked on the enormous bull, Buck sensed that something was shifting in the natural order around him. He could detect a new energy stirring throughout the land. Just as the moose had arrived in this territory, other forms of life were also moving in. The forest, streams, and very air itself seemed to pulse with their presence. This awareness came to him not through what he could see, hear, or smell, but through some deeper, more mysterious sense. Though he heard nothing and saw nothing concrete, he knew with certainty that the land had somehow transformed, that strange creatures were moving through it and establishing their territory, and he decided he would explore this phenomenon once he had completed the task at hand.

At last, at the end of the fourth day, he brought down the massive moose. For a full day and night he stayed beside his kill, alternating between eating and sleeping. Then, rested, refreshed and strong, he turned toward camp and John Thornton. He began his long, effortless stride, continuing hour after hour, never losing his way through the complex terrain, heading directly home through unfamiliar territory with a sense of direction that made man and his compass seem inadequate by comparison.

As he continued forward, he became increasingly aware of the new energy stirring throughout the land. A different kind of life pulsed through it now, unlike what had existed during the summer months. This awareness no longer came to him through vague, mysterious sensations. The birds spoke of it, the squirrels chattered about it, and even the gentle breeze carried whispers of it. Multiple times he paused to take deep breaths of the crisp morning air, interpreting a message that urged him to move forward with even greater urgency. He felt weighed down by the sense that disaster was approaching, or perhaps had already struck; and as he crossed the final ridge and descended into the valley toward camp, he moved with increased wariness.

Three miles away, he discovered a fresh trail that made the hair on his neck stand up and bristle. The trail led directly toward camp and John Thornton. Buck pressed forward quickly and quietly, every nerve stretched tight and alert to the countless details that told a story—everything except how it would end. His nose provided him with a changing account of the life that had passed along the path he was following. He noticed the heavy silence that filled the forest. The birds had disappeared. The squirrels were hiding. He spotted only one—a smooth gray creature pressed flat against a gray dead branch, making it look like part of the limb itself, like a natural growth on the wood.

As Buck moved through the darkness like a drifting shadow, his nose suddenly snapped to one side as if an invisible force had seized and yanked it. He tracked the fresh scent into a dense cluster of bushes and discovered Nig. The dog lay on his side, lifeless in the spot where he had crawled, with an arrow piercing completely through his body, its point and feathers visible on both sides.

A hundred yards ahead, Buck discovered one of the sled dogs that Thornton had purchased in Dawson. The dog was writhing in its final moments, right there on the trail, and Buck walked around it without pausing. From the camp drifted the distant sound of multiple voices, rising and falling in a rhythmic chant. Crawling forward on his belly to the edge of the clearing, he discovered Hans lying face down, bristling with arrows like a porcupine. At that very moment Buck looked toward where the spruce-bough shelter had stood and witnessed something that made the hair on his neck and shoulders stand straight up. A wave of overwhelming fury washed over him. He was unaware that he was growling, but he growled out loud with terrifying savagery. For the final time in his life he let emotion override cleverness and logic, and it was his deep love for John Thornton that caused him to lose control.

The Yeehats were dancing around the ruins of the spruce-bough lodge when they heard a terrifying roar and saw an animal unlike anything they had ever encountered charging toward them. It was Buck, a living storm of rage, throwing himself at them with wild fury bent on destruction. He leaped at the man in front (who was the Yeehat chief), tearing his throat wide open until the severed jugular gushed blood like a fountain. He didn't stop to worry over his victim, but slashed as he moved past, and with his next leap ripped open the throat of a second man. Nothing could stand against him. He dove into their midst, clawing, tearing, and destroying with relentless and terrible speed that made their arrows useless against him. His movements were so incredibly fast, and the Indians were packed so tightly together, that they ended up shooting each other with their own arrows; one young hunter, throwing a spear at Buck while he was in midair, drove it through another hunter's chest with such power that the point pierced through the skin of his back and protruded beyond. Then panic gripped the Yeehats, and they ran in terror into the woods, crying out as they fled about the coming of the Evil Spirit.

Buck truly became a demon in flesh, pursuing them relentlessly and bringing them down like hunted deer as they fled through the forest. This proved to be a devastating day for the Yeehats. They dispersed across the vast wilderness, and only after a full week did the remaining survivors finally regroup in a distant valley to assess their casualties. Growing tired of the chase, Buck eventually made his way back to the ravaged campsite. There he discovered Pete's body, still wrapped in his blankets where he had been struck down in those first shocking moments of the attack. The ground bore fresh evidence of Thornton's fierce battle for survival, and Buck carefully examined every trace of the struggle, following it all the way to the rim of a deep pool. At the water's edge, with his head and front paws submerged, lay Skeet, loyal until his final breath. The pool itself, clouded and murky from the mining equipment, concealed what lay beneath its surface, and within those depths rested John Thornton; Buck had tracked his scent into the water, but no trail emerged from the other side.

All day Buck brooded by the pool or wandered restlessly around the camp. He understood death as the end of movement, as departing from the world of the living, and he knew John Thornton was dead. This left an enormous emptiness inside him, similar to hunger, but a hollow ache that persisted and couldn't be satisfied by food. Sometimes, when he stopped to examine the bodies of the Yeehats, he temporarily forgot his pain; during these moments he felt an immense pride in himself—a pride greater than anything he had ever experienced before. He had killed humans, the most challenging prey of all, and he had done so despite the law of violence and brutality. He sniffed at the corpses with curiosity. They had died so effortlessly. Killing a husky dog was more difficult than killing them. They were completely outmatched, except for their arrows and spears and clubs. From now on he would fear them only when they carried their arrows, spears, and clubs in their hands.

Night fell, and a full moon climbed high above the trees into the sky, illuminating the landscape until it was bathed in an eerie daylight. With the arrival of darkness, as he brooded and grieved by the pool, Buck became aware of a stirring of new life in the forest beyond what the Yeehats had created. He rose to his feet, listening and sniffing the air. From a great distance came a faint, sharp howl, followed by a chorus of similar sharp howls. As time passed, the howls grew nearer and louder. Once again, Buck recognized them as sounds he had heard in that other world that remained alive in his memory. He walked to the center of the clearing and listened carefully. It was the call, the complex call, sounding more enticing and irresistible than it ever had before. And unlike ever before, he was prepared to answer it. John Thornton was dead. The final bond had been severed. Humanity and the demands of civilization no longer held him captive.

Hunting for fresh prey, just as the Yeehats were pursuing it along the edges of the migrating moose herds, the wolf pack had finally crossed over from the territory of rivers and forests and entered Buck's valley. They flowed into the moonlit clearing like a silver river, and there in the center of the open space stood Buck, still as a statue, waiting for their approach. The wolves were struck with awe at how motionless and massive he appeared, and a brief silence fell over them until the most daring wolf lunged directly at him. Swift as lightning, Buck attacked, snapping the wolf's neck. Then he resumed his position, completely still as before, while the wounded wolf writhed in pain behind him. Three more wolves attempted the same attack one right after another, and each one retreated, blood streaming from torn throats or shoulders.

This was enough to send the entire pack charging forward in a chaotic rush, packed together and tangled up in their frantic desire to bring down their target. Buck's incredible speed and nimbleness served him well. Spinning on his back legs while snapping and slashing, he seemed to be everywhere simultaneously, maintaining what appeared to be an unbroken defense line as he whirled and protected himself from every direction. However, to keep them from circling behind him, he was pushed backward, past the pool and down into the creek bed, until he found himself against a steep gravel embankment. He maneuvered along until he reached a corner in the bank that miners had carved out during their work, and in this corner he made his stand, shielded on three sides with only the front to defend.

He handled the confrontation so effectively that after thirty minutes, the wolves retreated in defeat. All their tongues hung out, panting heavily, while their white fangs gleamed menacingly in the moonlight. Some wolves lay on the ground with their heads up and ears alert, others remained standing as they watched him, and still others were drinking from the water pool. One wolf, tall and slender with gray fur, approached carefully in a non-threatening way, and Buck recognized his wild companion from their night and day of running together. The wolf made soft whining sounds, and when Buck whined back, they gently touched noses.

Then an old wolf, thin and marked by many battles, stepped forward. Buck curled his lips in the beginning of a snarl, but touched noses with the wolf. After this, the old wolf sat down, pointed his nose toward the moon, and let out the long howl of his kind. The other wolves sat down and howled as well. And now the call reached Buck with clear meaning. He also sat down and howled. When this was finished, he moved out from his position and the pack gathered around him, sniffing in a way that was both friendly and wild. The lead wolves gave the sharp cry of the pack and leaped away into the forest. The wolves followed behind them, crying out together. And Buck ran alongside them, next to his wild brother, calling out as he ran.

And here the story of Buck could very well come to an end. It wasn't many years before the Yeehats began to notice changes in the breed of timber wolves; some were spotted with patches of brown on their heads and snouts, along with a streak of white running down the center of their chests. Even more extraordinary than this, the Yeehats speak of a Ghost Dog that leads the pack. They fear this

Ghost Dog, for it possesses greater intelligence than they do, stealing from their camps during harsh winters, raiding their traps, killing their dogs, and challenging their most courageous hunters.

No, the story becomes even more disturbing. There are hunters who never make it back to camp, and there have been hunters whose fellow tribesmen discovered them with their throats brutally torn open, surrounded by wolf tracks in the snow that were larger than those of any ordinary wolf. Every autumn, when the Yeehats follow the migrating moose, there is one particular valley they refuse to enter. And there are women who grow sorrowful when stories are told around the fire about how the Evil Spirit chose that valley as its dwelling place.

In the summers there is one visitor, however, to that valley, of which the Yeehats do not know. It is a great, magnificently coated wolf, like, and yet unlike, all other wolves. He travels alone from the cheerful timber land and comes down into an open space among the trees. Here a yellow stream flows from rotted moose-hide sacks and sinks into the ground, with long grasses growing through it and plant matter covering it and hiding its yellow from the sun; and here he reflects for a time, howling once, long and sorrowfully, before he leaves.

But he isn't always by himself. When the long winter nights arrive and the wolves chase their prey down into the lower valleys, you might spot him running at the front of the pack through the pale moonlight or shimmering northern lights, jumping enormous distances above his companions, his massive throat bellowing as he sings a song of the ancient world, which is the song of the pack.

THE END

Thank You For Reading

You've Just Read a Piece of the Greatest Library Ever Rebuilt

Thank you for reading.

This book is one of thousands we're restoring, reimagining, and translating as part of the **Modern Library of Alexandria** — a global movement to preserve and share humanity's most important ideas.

What was once lost to fire and time is now rising again — not just as memory, but as living, breathing knowledge, freely accessible to all.

What You Can Do Next:

*   **Keep Reading.**

    Discover more legendary works — in beautiful print, audiobook, or digital form — at LibraryofAlexandria.com.

*   **Build Your Own Library.**

    Every title is available as a paperback, hardcover, or collectible boxset — at true printing cost. Craft a personal library worthy of display.

*   **Spread the Light.**

    Share this book. Tell others about the movement. Help us translate every timeless work into every language, so no reader is ever left behind.

By finishing this book, you've already taken part in something extraordinary.

Join us at LibraryofAlexandria.com

Together, we're rebuilding the greatest library the world has ever known.

With appreciation,

The Modern Library of Alexandria Team

Visit:
www.libraryofalexandria.com
Or scan the code below: